About the Author

The author has a degree in Applied Biology and Biopharmaceutical Science and a Masters in Health Promotion Practice. She enjoys spending time with her dogs, playing drums and farming sheep. She loves reading and gets the inspiration for writing from reading other genres.

The Games We Play

S M Murray

The Games We Play

Olympia Publishers
London

www.olympiapublishers.com
OLYMPIA PAPERBACK EDITION

Copyright © S M Murray 2024

The right of S M Murray to be identified as author of
this work has been asserted in accordance with sections 77 and 78 of
the Copyright, Designs and Patents Act 1988.

All Rights Reserved

No reproduction, copy or transmission of this publication
may be made without written permission.
No paragraph of this publication may be reproduced,
copied or transmitted save with the written permission of the publisher,
or in accordance with the provisions
of the Copyright Act 1956 (as amended).

Any person who commits any unauthorised act in relation to
this publication may be liable to criminal
prosecution and civil claims for damage.

A CIP catalogue record for this title is
available from the British Library.

ISBN: 978-1-80439-818-0

This is a work of fiction.
The names, places and people in this book are fiction and used for the
purpose of telling this story.

First Published in 2024

Olympia Publishers
Tallis House
2 Tallis Street
London
EC4Y 0AB

Printed in Great Britain

Prologue

I see her in the bar, I know she doesn't like me. She never has and she doesn't shy away from her distaste towards me. She'll look directly at me and turn away just to make a point. I suppose one can't be liked by everyone and maybe I deserve it.

I saw her at a party once and wondered what she was doing out. Maybe, in my drunken state I said that to her and may have said more and appeared ignorant – not a great first impression, I'll admit. They say sober thoughts lead to drunken words. I can't remember much about that night but from what I've seen in her expression towards me, it's safe to assume she definitely remembers that night.

Maybe it's boredom or maybe it's for pleasure, but I think I like the challenge of getting her to like me or at least tolerate me. Then slowly let her think I'm a nice guy and she just met me on a bad night back then.

Then this can lead to trust and maybe more (women can be so predictable – that whole "I'm a nice man deep down, just give me a chance" works every time.) Women always think they can change a man, especially if he's good looking and I know I am. I've had my fair share of one-night stands to prove it. They all leave me their number with a coy smile after thinking, *actually* hoping, I'll call, but I never do. Names I can't even remember. I know I've slept with a few Michelles but that's the only name I can remember because it's my sister's name. The lads call me the hammer. Why? Because of all the girls I've nailed. I'm a legend among the lads.

I've never had a girlfriend because that monogamy crap does not appeal to me at all. I like pulling too much. I enjoy the flirting, the flattery I present to a woman to make her think she is the only one I want to engage in conversation with and she is… for that night, anyway. The usual stuff I ask "What do you do", "How many are in your family" and that leads to a family story. I always order another drink when that conversation starts, *bla bla bla*. Then the usual looking into her eyes and smiling and after that, they are mine for the night. Being good-looking really does have its advantages; I mean, come on, if I were heavy and small with greasy hair and spots, would girls really look at me? So, it's not being cocky by stating the obvious. Like I said, the number of girls in my bed proves this. Thankfully no STIs because, of course, I would have to get tested; I mean, even a real hammer needs a clean.

But one can get bored of that. Well, not bored but just need a break from it. It wasn't my plan to go looking for Tara Whelan as a new personal project, I just saw her that night and thought, well, this is something new and a plan came to mind. Why did I decide to do it? Well, I thought, why not?

When I'm done with her, she will be left broken and would have regretted ever getting to know me. She should have stuck with her first impression of me. She'll beat herself over this for a long time.

But by then, I would have had my fun.

Let the game begin.

Chapter One

Tom suggests we change the scenery tonight and go to a different pub. 'I think you have probably gone home with all the women in our usual pubs by now, Ciaran,' laughs Tom. He's not wrong. I probably have, not being cocky but we do drink in our usual pubs nearly every weekend and I never go home alone. Sometimes, it has ended with me bringing home the same girl a few times and still forgetting her name. Lately, I have gotten a few bad looks from the girls in the pub and noticed them whispering to each other, but by the end of the night, other girls are smiling with me and I get to pick who the lucky girl is going to come home with me that night. They are always hoping for more the next morning – will they ever learn? The word has to have gotten around about me and monogamy but still, they think they will be the one to change me. *Pffft!*

I don't mind going to a different pub. Fresh faces are always good for the self-esteem. Instead of walking like we normally do, we have to get a taxi to this pub that Tom suggested. I hate this because it means waiting ages for a taxi at the end of the night. But I'm not going to complain because as discussed, change is good.

We get to the pub. It's a lot quieter than our usual. A lot of faces I do not recognise which is mostly to do with the ages. They are all mostly in their 50s. While I do like women, I have to draw the line at some age. I look at Tom to suggest that I won't be pulling tonight. He looks at me; three years of living together, he definitely knows what I'm thinking and laughs.

There's a nice niche across the bar. We all go over and sit and Tom gets the drinks in. The four of us are looking around the pub like hunters looking for our prey. It's a cosy pub, there's a fireplace in the far corner with a blaring fire alight in it. The walls look freshly painted which suggests either a new owner or new construction.

I never thought to ask Tom how he heard about this place. I'm assuming from work. And, of course, I am right because in walks two of his colleagues and they see Tom and head straight over to him. They both have the same haircut; a side split and swept back. Even if I didn't know them, by just looking at their haircuts anyone would know that they are solicitors.

The three of them come over together with a pint in their hands, Tom having brought over one drops it on the table and heads back for the rest. I get up and help him. Well... I take my own pint, but it's still helping because he doesn't have go to back a third time.

Something or someone catches my eye as I grab my pint at the bar. It looks like Tara Whelan. She is talking with two other girls.

She has brown hair but it's pinned up in a way only a hairdresser could achieve. She's wearing a lace navy dress. She's smaller than the other two girls but when I look at the floor, I see that she's wearing low heels whereas the other two girls are wearing platform shoes. I would not want to run in those shoes or walk either. They look so uncomfortable. One of the many good things about being a lad is comfy shoes all day and night.

While looking at their shoes and admiring my traits, I notice the girl turn her head towards the door. I get a better view of her face. Yep! It is Tara Whelan. That girl hates me! I forget why.

Well, I never really knew why, but I always remember those eyes when they look at me when I'm home at Christmas. They are like daggers.

She doesn't see me. I just grab my pint and head back to the table with the lads. I'm sitting in a good position. I can talk to the boys and see Tara and her friends. As usual, they are drinking their gin and tonics with the big goblin glasses. Never understood the point of them big glasses! What are they doing in this pub? They seem to know the bartender as the three of them have been laughing and chatting to him since they came in.

She still hasn't looked over this way. I should be angry that she doesn't feel my presence, but it's quite nice to see she can smile when I'm not in her sight.

One of Tom's friends Jason is bragging about a case he won earlier today. It sounds like it was an easy case to win anyway; something about burglary and the burglar was seen on the CCTV so there wasn't much work involved for prosecution. Anyway, I'm not really listening, I'm just drinking my pint and nodding every now and again. But what I am thinking is how to have fun with Tara because I will probably never see her again, I haven't seen her for the last two Christmases and I kind of missed the dagger looks. I always take great pleasure in those slaughtering eyes.

I can sort of remember the first night seeing her and I was thinking, *What is this young one doing at this party?* I was quite drunk so maybe I went over to her and asked her that question and maybe I said more ignorant things too, but I can't remember.

Drink always makes you say things that you are thinking so I'm assuming I did *just* that.

I saw her again a few weeks later and the look on her face

that night actually haunted me, for a few hours anyway. So that confirmed it. I did talk to her. Maybe one day I will ask her what I said but over the last few years, I suppose I did enjoy wondering if and when she saw me, what way would she look at me. Every time, she never lets me down. Those eyes are like daggers going straight into my head. If looks could kill, I would definitely have a painful and prolonged death.

I have finished my pint so I am going to head to the toilets. As I walk past, she still doesn't see me. Her back is turned. *Damn!*

I'm taking my time in the toilets and I know I need another pint so I will go to the bar now.

I walk slowly out to the bar and I notice that all three women are gone. Damn again! I go to the bar and order another pint. I'm pondering what to do here because Tom bought the last round but now, I will have to buy his friends drinks too. It would be rude not to, but I don't know them that well. Oh, I better just do it. It's only an extra tenner anyway. Then that's my part done. I won't be buying any girls drinks tonight anyway, unless I'm in the mood for a cougar.

Jason and Marcus are very grateful. I do my usual gracious act of no bother. Tom knows it very well because he gives me a coy smile. As I'm heading back to the bar for two more pints, I see the three girls coming out of the bathroom. Ah! Tara sees me. She instantly goes from smiling to that famous dagger look that she retains just for me. Well, it's nice to know that she remembers me and even better to know that she will always save that slaughtering stare just for me. Lucky me!

I still have two more pints to collect from the bar so I walk back but nothing from her this time. Her back is turned. The two girls aren't looking my way. She obviously didn't tell them our history. Should I be flattered or offended?

Well, it looks like I'm not going anywhere for a while because Jason just bought another round. I normally go through pints like water, but tonight I am taking my time drinking them.

I'm curious to know why we are in this pub. So, I ask Jason if he drinks here much. Jason smiles and says, 'Yeah, we come here for a few quiet drinks, but I told Tom to come here tonight because Megan, a girl that works across from our office, is having her sister's hen tonight and she said they were starting here because their uncle owns the bar.'

I look at Tom with my mouth open. 'Oh a woman has led us all to change from our usual pubs. Well, that is something.'

Tom looks mortified. He hates it when I tease him about women because he is no way near as comfortable around women as I am. Yes, I'm arrogant, but it's part of my charm and I've never received any complaints from the women, until the next day anyway. But by then I have forgotten their names so it doesn't bother me.

'So, are we here early drinking so Tom can strike up some Dutch courage to talk to Megan?' I smile at Tom but he still looks embarrassed. I can be such a prick. The boys all laugh.

'Ah, I'm only joking. You know me; I can be a prick at times. This is great for you, Tom. Seriously! So, when are they coming?' I look at Jason and Marcus for the answer.

'I think Megan said half nine but women are always late so who knows.' Jason hunches his shoulders and drinks his pint.

I am happy for Tom, he deserves to have a girlfriend. He has all the characteristics of a boyfriend, unlike me. He's loyal, good-natured and considerate. He would've had a lot of girlfriends only he's so damn self-conscious. Drink helps him come out of his shell so it makes sense that we are here before the hen party.

That must be why Tara is here. I'm assuming the older bartender is Megan's uncle and the younger one is his son.

Just as Conor is bringing the pints over, the main door flies open and in walk about ten girls. But judging solely by the noise they're making, one would think fifty girls walked in. I see some in pink hats and hairbands and, of course, a typical bride is wearing a white veil and white dress. She's tall with blonde hair. She's either a natural blonde or she just got it dyed because she doesn't have dark roots. Even if she wasn't wearing white, she would still stand out because she's the only blonde. The other girls have a mixture of brown, black and red hair. I could try pulling her tonight, but she's Megan's sister. I don't think Tom would be happy with me if I messed this up for him. But some harmless flirting wouldn't damage Tom's chances with Megan.

Tara and her two friends are hugging the rest of the hen party. They are acting like they haven't seen each other in years and they probably all saw one another yesterday. So ridiculous!

A cute brunette looks over at our table and smiles. That must be Megan! I look at Tom and his face looks anxious. He is drinking his pint fast; giving himself some of that Dutch courage. She is saying something to the bride and then walks towards our table. She's wearing a black dress with a sash that says BRIDESMAID on it. She is cute, but I have limits. Besides, there is plenty to choose from tonight. Hen parties are always fun because they all love the attention. One can almost smell the desperation. It smells mostly of La Vie est Belle or sometimes Dior.

'Hey, Tom! Jason! Marcus! How are ye?' She makes eye contact with us all as she says it. I stand to make my introduction. I can be a gentleman when I want to be and I'm doing this for Tom.

'Hi, I'm Ciaran. I live with Tom.' I smile and shake her hand. Megan smiles back. I face the other three lads. 'This is Conor, he also lives with me and Tom and this is Finn and Oliver, they do not live with us.' A little light humour! It works because they all laugh.

'So, it's your sister's hen tonight,' Tom says while looking over at the party.

'Yeah, it is. Well… it's a party but not a hen party.'

She sees us look at her sash and corrects herself. 'Oh yeah, I know, we are only wearing these sashes in here because our uncle owns the pub. We thought we could be silly in here but we're leaving everything *HEN* in this pub and then heading to a few others for drinks. My sister doesn't like the attention a hen party brings.' She gives a coy and obvious smile to us all to indicate it's the men's attention that bothers her sister at the hen parties. Tom looks directly at me. I get the message loud and clear. Have manners tonight.

Megan continues saying, 'So, at least in here she can get comfortable attention with people she knows and then when we leave, it'll be off her. She's hoping anyway,' laughs Megan. 'Are ye here for the night or are ye going somewhere?' She's looking at Tom as she says this. I don't know if she's hoping we'll follow them or just making conversation.

But Tom makes the decision. 'Yeah, here for another while anyway. We have a few more rounds to go. I have to buy my round yet.'

The liar! He bought the first round. It looks like we will be staying for as long as they are staying.

Megan smiles. She seems pleased. 'Oh great,' Megan looks over at the girls; one of them nods with a drink in the air, indicating it's Megan's. 'Well, I will chat to ye later. I better go back to the party. Nice meeting ye.' She looks at us all and then gives one more look to Tom and heads back to the party. Tom seems pleased too.

It's obvious they are both interested in each other. Would they hurry it up already?

'Oh, she likes you, Tom.' I have to be the one to announce it.

'Yeah, she is nice,' says Tom.

'So, what is taking you so long to make the move? You have a few pints in you now. Move it!' I say eagerly.

'No, not tonight. She's with her sister and that's her uncle behind the bar. Too much family in one place.'

'Yeah, fair enough. Well, you better talk to her more before the night is over and maybe ask her out.' I give him the elbow as I say it.

'I will,' Tom says assertively. Hopefully, he will. But maybe he needs more alcohol to hurry this process along.

'I think it's time for shots. I'll be right back, lads.'

I'm such a good friend.

*

We have all started mingling with the hen party. Tom and Megan haven't stopped talking to one another.

In some situations, alcohol can have its benefits. In this case, it helps a shy man become confident around a girl he likes.

Some of the hens I have engaged in conversation with tell me about their husbands and children. Boring! Three others are single and after talking to them, I'm starting to see why. Boring! Then there's Tara who is keeping her distance from me but when any eye contact is made, it's with those hateful eyes saved just for me.

Ah, feck it! I'm going over to her. Oh My God! I actually feel sick. Is that the shots mixing with the pints or am I scared to talk to her?

She's talking to the bride and sees me walking over to them. She's stunned. I know it. She doesn't know whether to leave or stay. I keep walking.

'Hi. How are you? You must be the bride.' I smile at them both. Tara just looks at me. Her eyes change from anger to confusion.

I keep smiling and the bride smiles back, saying, 'Yeah, I'm the bride, my name is Rachel and this is Tara.'

Tara still just looks at me. Rachel looks confused as to why Tara didn't smile when she introduced her to me. I may as well state the obvious. 'Yeah, me and Tara know each other. We are both from the same place.' Rachel turns to Tara, smiling. 'Oh wow, really? The same place, what are the chances?'

Tara finally speaks. (I don't think I ever heard her voice) 'Yeah, we are from the same place, unfortunately.'

I tilt my head towards Rachel. 'Yeah. Tara doesn't like me. I don't really know why.'

Oh, alcohol, sometimes you are a curse.

Rachel's mouth goes from wide to an oval shape. The tension is bad now but Tara doesn't give in.

'YEAH, I don't like you. I think you are rude and arrogant and I don't know where you get this opinion of yourself. You haven't ended world hunger so why so obnoxious?'

Rachel makes a sympathetic face but Tara just looks at her and then back to me. 'Well, he asked so I think I owe him to give my honest opinion no matter how harsh it is.' She looks at me and states what I already know. But it's nice to be told again just in case her tone wasn't clear. 'I don't like you.' She leaves her glass down and looks at Rachel and gives me one last stare then says, 'I'm going to the bathroom.'

I look at Rachel and make a whistling noise. 'As you can see, we have a past.'

'Yeah, it seems the two of ye have a bad past. Did ye go out?'

'No! No! No! I think I was rude to her one night. I was drunk so I don't remember what I said, but obviously, she does. But yeah, then I remember one night seeing her out and she just glared at me and I knew that I definitely said something to her on a previous night. Maybe she'll tell you because I really can't remember.'

'Well, it must be bad given the fact she didn't even try to be polite to you even in front of me,' states Rachel.

Thank you for stating the obvious.

'Yeah. I know,' I say anxiously.

I'm trying to control my emotions because I'm delighted I shocked her.

That was fun! I wonder how much fun it will be if I keep pursuing her. It might really get on her nerves if I mingle with more of the hen party.

I could have some fun too.

Hmmmm! I feel a plan coming along. I'd rub my chin only people would notice that I'm up to something, especially Tom. I could talk to all the women at this party and make out like I'm this self-conscious shy man and have them question Tara's perception of me. I could also go a bit further and make Tara think her first impression of me was wrong. Well, not wrong but that I've changed from who I was back then.

I could make her think she is wrong about me now. Even

though I'm exactly the same as I was, only a bit older and better looking. It could be a big challenge but one I'm willing to accept. It's always good to challenge oneself. Keep the brain active. I'm a changed man and am willing to make amends for whatever I said that upset her or angered her every time she saw me since *that* night.

This could be fun. Everyone gets itchy feet and my feet have been scratched a lot over the years, maybe I need a different sort of itch. Teachers, nurses, even guards take a career break to refresh themselves. This is what I need to do.

I need to refresh myself.

The one-night stands were entertaining but now this will be a different sort of entertainment but still very entertaining. I need to stop saying entertaining!

First things first. Buy her a drink. They all seem to love that goblin glass crap. I'll order that. But I remember actually I saw her with a normal glass so they either ran out of those glasses which could happen, it's not a very busy pub, or she is drinking Vodka. I'm chancing that.

'Hi, can I have a pint of Carlsberg and vodka white? Thanks.' The bartender and I exchange pleasantries. I state that my friends and I are not part of the hen party. We will not be dancing or taking our clothes off no matter how much alcohol we consume.

He responds by saying, 'That's good because some of the older gentlemen would die of shock to see that sort of entertainment in here. We'd lose a lot of valuable patrons and bills have to be paid. Rachel doesn't like any of that. She'd probably leave her own party if she suspected anything like that was going to happen.' He leaves the glass of vodka and the bottle of white lemonade on the bar.

I look at him curiously. I know they are cousins but it would be weird if I said 'Oh yes, I know you two are cousins even though ye are two strangers to me.'

Best to stick with the facial expression for an explanation.

'Oh sorry! I'm Brian, the bride's cousin.' He points to Rachel as he says it. I look to see who he's talking about.

'*Ahhh!*' My face says it all. I'm reassured by his explanation.

'Yeah. My father owns this pub.' He looks over at his father talking to a couple at the other side of the bar.

I look around at the bar with interest. 'Yeah. It's a nice pub. Very homely! Do ye have it long?'

'Yeah. We have had it for about ten years. We had to do a bit of construction last year because a water pipe burst. So, we have been reopened again for about four months.'

That explains the paint job I noticed earlier.

'Oh right. Yeah, water can be just as damaging as fire. Messy too,' I add with empathy.

As he's pulling my pint, he adds, 'Oh yeah. We would have got screwed on the insurance too only for the assessor we hired. He was brilliant.'

'Oh wow! Lucky ye thought of getting one. Some people don't think about doing that. Did ye look for him or hear about him?'

'Yeah, Rachel's soon-to-be sister-in-law recommended him to us. She got him when there was a fire incident at her coffee shop. Now here's your pint.' He places it in front of me.

'Thanks. Right. Well, glad it worked out and ye are open again.'

'Yeah. Thanks.' I pour some of the white lemonade into the glass and take the two drinks.

I look around the pub. *Ah*, there's Tara! She's talking to

Megan.

I'm looking around for Tom and he is talking to Rachel. *Awh*, that's nice, he's meeting the family. He'd kill me if I said that now. But I won't, I'm a good friend. Tonight, Tara and her lovely, hateful eyes have my full attention. So, it begins.

'Hey, Megan! Hi, Tara! I bought you a drink. Vodka white. I noticed your glass and assumed that's what you were drinking. Am I right?'

Tara looks questionably at Megan. She doesn't want to take the drink. She wants to embarrass me. But Megan smiles and gives Tara a look that I'm assuming insinuates that she "play nice".

Tara looks at me and reluctantly takes the drink and says 'Thanks.'

Oh, that must have killed her to say that to me. I feel her pain. This situation is painful for me too. God bless Megan for being here and ensuring there is a bit of pleasantry in this tense atmosphere.

I'm mostly interacting with Megan who is telling me about her sister's wedding. She's talking about what they have done for it and what jobs still need to be done.

Rachel's ears must have been burning because she walks over smiling, wanting to join the conversation. I'm not really listening, just smiling and nodding, I hope she doesn't expect me to ask follow-up questions about the wedding because I might ask a question that she already answered and then I would be in trouble. When I see her lips have stopped moving, I try to bring Tara into the conversation.

'I know ye are sisters. But how do ye know Tara? Is it from college or work?' I try and stop myself from smiling so I look at the floor and then I look at Megan and Rachel and give a quick glance to Tara. I don't really care how they know Tara, but I need to engage with her someway.

All three look at each other. Tara says nothing and keeps her face expressionless. One can always depend on the bride in these situations to start the conversation flowing again. Rachel smiles, here comes the big pointless story. It's never easy with women; they can't just say yes, we work together; it has to be a story. I refrain from rolling my eyes while Rachel starts.

'Tara is going to be my sister-in-law. I met my fiancé…'

Fiancé! *Pffft!*

I hate when they say that. Are they bragging that they have a fiancé and I should be jealous of it? I don't know nor do I care. She's still talking, but I trailed off. Better turn on the ears now. I'm catching the end of the story.

'… and then he finally asked me out and now here we are three years later about to be married.'

I look at Tara. She looks as bored as I feel. Well, there's one thing we have in common. We don't care about the love story of other people's lives. I'm hoping I'm hiding my boredom better than she is.

Rachel doesn't even notice. She's too busy thinking and talking about herself. The other girls must hear Rachel talking about the wedding because three of them come over and join us. The three of them are married already so they seem to enjoy all that wedding talk. It gives them an excuse to talk about their wedding days. I'm stuck between six women listening to them talk about weddings I could care less about. I need to leave but I'm stuck. I have one either side of me and they think they are considerate by making eye contact with me as well as the other girls when they are telling their stories. It would be more considerate if they allowed me to walk away.

Wait, there are only five ladies now. Where did Tara go? Oh, that sneaky bitch, she must have seen an opportunity and took it. Well, the only way I can get out of this is to go to the toilet. So, I finish my pint while smiling at the ladies. I excuse myself about the 'call of nature'. Don't think they noticed but I'm covered in case they think I was rude to just walk away. I better head to the toilet and not make a liar out of myself.

I'm about to turn the corner in the direction of the toilets when...

BANG! Ouuuuuch!

My head! Is that my echo? I open my eyes and see Tara with a hand on her forehead and her eyes closed. An exact imitation of myself, just a different sex.

Ouch! This is sore!

The bitch!

She was waiting for her opportunity to hit me. Hope it was worth it because it fucking hurts.

'What the fuck? Do you not look where you are going? Or is your ego that big that you can't see in front of you!' shouts Tara.

Feck her! This wasn't my fault. 'What? You are blaming me for this! What about you? Could you not see in front of you because you are so high on your pedestal?' I shout back.

I can be angry too.

Tara looks angry. 'Ou! This fucking hurts!'

'Yeah, well, so does mine. I know it's hard to believe but I think this was an accident on both our parts.' My eyes are closed while I'm saying this.

The pain! I open my eyes and keep my hand to my forehead.

She looks at me, her hand still on her forehead and a smile seems to form. 'Yeah, maybe, think I need a drink after that to numb this fucking pain.'

She walks past me fast. It's so fast I can feel a breeze go through me.

I walk back into the bar and find myself looking for Tara. Not because I'm concerned about her, I just want to see if there's a bruise on her head. I checked mine in the bathroom and I have a bright red mark just above my eyebrow. It is so sore.

I see her talking to Tom and Megan. She's probably telling them it was my fault. I can't see any mark on her head. I need to get a closer look.

I'll add a bit of humour.

'Hi, Tara! How's your head?' She just looks at me with fury and then slowly her mouth forms a smile. I can see the mark now. There's a bit of a bump on her forehead. It does look sore.

'Yeah, it's still quite sore but I think a few more of these' – she holds up her glass – 'and I should not feel the pain and probably not remember the night.'

I'm wondering were the last few words meant for my benefit? She doesn't want to remember meeting me. Well, I will make sure she does remember me.

She takes a sip of her drink and asks, 'How's your head? OOOOH, it looks sore. It's red.'

I put my hand to my head and wince. 'Yeah, it is.'

Tom interrupts, saying, 'Yeah, Tara was telling us ye bumped heads going to the bathroom.'

'More like banged heads by the way we look and feel,' I say. Megan and Tom both look at our heads and start to laugh. I suppose we do look ridiculous. I would laugh too if it wasn't me in this situation.

'I think I'll follow your lead, Tara, and get a drink.'

I order a double whiskey. Normally, I don't drink whiskey

but people have hot whiskey to calm their nerves so I figure a double will numb the pain.

As I'm sipping my whiskey, I realise this is the perfect excuse to strike up a conversation with Tara. We can talk about the pain, not that I care about her pain, but if it gets her talking to me, then I will take it.

I order another whiskey and a vodka for Tara. I suppose it's the gentleman thing to do. I might get too drunk to stick to my plan. But I'll try not to. I can't. I will just sip my whiskey. My plan will distract me from the pain.

I see Tara with one of the boring single girls. This is a good opportunity. I grab the two glasses and head over.

'Hey, Tara!' I show her the glass of vodka. 'This is a little peace offering and an apology for hurting your head.' I place it in front of her. She hesitates for a moment and then decides to take it. I don't think she wants to appear rude in front of Sadie (I think her name is).

She says 'Thanks. But it was my fault too.'

Jackpot! She's taking responsibility for some of the incident. She's warming to me.

'Well, then, the next drinks are on you.' I laugh and so do Sadie and Tara.

This is working. Now I just need Sadie to disappear.

I hear Rachel shout a name and Sadie looks over. OK, so her name is Sandra. I was close. They both begin with S.

Sandra then looks at me and Tara and says 'Sorry, I'll be back. I think Rachel wants me for something.' She smiles and leaves us. So now it is just the two of us.

Time to put on the act of you don't know the real me. A sensitive and kind man who just needs someone to give him a chance. I don't think Tara is going to start this conversation off, so I will just have to start.

'So, looks like you are stuck talking to an obnoxious me.' I smile warmly at my smart comment.

Tara looks at me with stern in her eyes. 'NO. I don't think so,' and walks away.

Oh crap, that sarcastic humour didn't work.

I walk after her quickly and say, 'Wait. Sorry, I thought my sarcastic comment would lighten the mood. Obviously not.'

She turns. 'Yeah, obviously not,' and keeps walking.

This is going to be hard. She joins Rachel and the other girls. I cannot give up now so easily besides this is quite entertaining for me. I take a few more sips of my whiskey and walk over to the ladies.

'Hi, ladies! Can I just have a quick word with Tara for a minute?' She looks at the girls for help, but they give her sympathetic looks that suggest 'hear him out anyway'. She lets out a sigh and walks with me to two free seats near the bar. She looks angry. I don't know why; I mean, I got hit in the forehead too.

'I'm sorry for the comment and your forehead and I'm sorry for the polar ice caps melting.'

She rolls her eyes at me.

'Apologies. Sarcastic humour again. It normally works, but I see this time it isn't so… that's the last of it. I can be very observant at times and I notice from your eye roll that you don't appreciate sarcastic comments.'

'No, I can appreciate them especially when it's me that makes them or other people.' She gives a sarcastic smile.

The irony of it all.

'Right. So, it's just sarcastic comments coming from me that bothers you.'

She just stares at me. Message received. Over time, she'll change her mind.

Time to put all those romance movies nonsense to the test. Must appear self-conscious and remorseful for any offence I caused her.

'Look, I probably won't see you again and I'm sure that is music to your ears, but just while I meet you on your own, I just want to apologise for anything I may have said or done to make you hate me so much. I mean obviously, we weren't friends that fell out. We never talked, at least not soberly anyway. I just remember seeing you at a party, I think.' I look at her for some recognition and she nods. Great, I was right about that part.

'And then I got dagger looks from you shortly after that, so I assumed I must have said something to you at that party. Something that definitely upset or offended you.'

Remorseful – check ✓

My body language is good too because I was moving my glass back and forth and I was keeping eye contact with her while talking but looking at the table at times to suggest I'm not confident in myself to keep looking at her.

Self-conscious – check ✓

I think I did it well but, of course, I'm going to be biased to my own performance. I think I will need to convince her more. Don't know if she bought it all.

She replies sternly, 'Yeah, you did. You were very rude to me, didn't even ask me my name or anything to strike up a polite conversation. You just came out with a rude comment followed by another one and then you laughed and went back to your friends. You seemed pleased with yourself and at that moment, I thought I never want to see him again. But then I did see you again and I thought yeah, I'm gonna let him know that I dislike him, hence "the lovely glances" I give you every time I see you.' She keeps a straight face.

From that response, she either doesn't believe my apology or doesn't care to hear it.

'Yeah, I know I've been told I can be an ass when I drink, ha, I can be an ass when I don't drink too.' I'm admitting to my bad behaviour without apologising for it.

'Yeah, I would believe it.' She takes a sip of the vodka that I bought for her. She trusts me enough to know that I didn't spit in it. Though I was tempted.

'Well, I can see I'm starting to get into your good books.'

'COME ON, GIRLS, MORE DRINK TO BE HAD IN THE NEXT PUB!' announces Rachel.

'Well, that's my cue.' She gets up from her seat to leave. More like jumps up to leave. Rachel timed it nicely for her, whether she meant to or not.

'Yeah, hope talking to me wasn't too much torture for you,' I say, keeping eye contact with her.

'No, it was fine.'

LIAR!

'Maybe next time I see you, you might smile at me.' I give a cheeky smile

'Yeah, maybe,' and she gives me a half smile. Progress!

I stand as she leaves; it's the gentlemanly thing to do.

'Ah, I'm taking that smile. That's progress.'

Oh no, I'm saying what's in my head. Thankfully, she is leaving before I drink any more. My ten-minute plan could have gone downhill very fast there.

She walks off towards the bride and the other girls. I keep smiling in case she turns back and… Yes! She does. She bought all that crap.

As soon as they are gone, the smile stays on my face but not because I liked talking to her. Definitely NOT! My plan is now in motion.

I walk over to Tom and the lads. Tom seems pleased with himself. I'm assuming he moved things along with Megan. Good for him!

Chapter Two

I'm eating pizza I ordered from our usual takeaway 'Marco's'. It's a Friday night and I didn't feel like cooking. I had parent-teacher meetings all week. Every year, I dread them more and more. It's all 'my son never has homework problems at home so how can he be doing badly in that subject?' and 'my daughter plays club camogie, can you give her less homework?'. Some parents can actually be more childish and challenging than their children.

Tom comes into the kitchen; he heads straight towards the fridge. He grabs two beers and hands me one.

'Oh, thanks. How was work? I got pizza if you want any.' I point to the box while finishing my third slice.

'Yeah, don't mind if I do.' He grabs a slice. 'Yeah, work was fine, how was the last of your meetings?'

'Yeah, I think the best were saved for last. They were really pleasant and supportive parents. The week started off bad and ended well. So, cheers to that.' We clink our beers.

'So, are you seeing Megan tonight?' I ask cheekily

Tom was on a few dates with Megan so it was fair to say they're starting to become an item. I'm happy for Tom.

'Yeah, I saw her for lunch today but not meeting her tonight. She's going out with friends from work. It's one of their birthdays. She asked me out tomorrow night with her family and a few friends for her sister's wedding. They're having a get-together because some of her family came from America for the wedding. She asked if you and Conor would like to come too.'

I squint my face. 'I don't know. I'm not really into that family meeting stuff and I wouldn't be able to get drunk to loosen up because it's a family thing.'

'Ah, please, come on. She did ask the two of ye and I don't want to go on my own. You'd be doing me a big favour.'

'*Hmmmmm*... I don't know.'

'Ah, come on. You're not doing anything and you had a hard week. It would do you good to go out after your suffering.'

'Wow, you must really need me to go with you to be sucking up to me.' I take a swig of my beer.

'Yeah, I do. I don't want to meet the family on my own. And if you come, I'll look like a gentleman,' laughs Tom. The prick!

'Haha, you're so funny. Think you've just convinced me not to go. Good luck!' I take another slice of pizza and smile at him.

'Ah, you know I'm messing. Come on. Please. I'll owe you.'

Seeing him grovel is so satisfying and he will owe me a favour. That will come in handy someday. I stay quiet and eat my pizza. Let him stew for a while.

'Is it because Tara will be there?'

I turn my head and look at him, confused at what he said.

'Tara? Why would she be there?'

'Ah, because Megan's sister is marrying her brother.' He rolls his eyes to insinuate that I should already know this. I had known, but forgotten.

'Oh yeah. I completely forgot about that.'

This is perfect. I was planning on 'accidentally' going into the coffee shop that Tara owns one day and planning (we met Megan at her uncle's pub one night and she told us all about the girls from the hen. I got Conor to ask that question to avoid suspicion from me) from there but this is perfect. It's sooner than

I planned but that doesn't mean it's bad timing.

'All right! Fine! I'll go.'

Tom smiles. 'Ah. Thanks, mate.'

'But you will owe me,' I say while finishing my last slice of pizza.

'Yes. Yes. Anything you want but within reason and legal.' He smiles, taking a sip of his beer.

Chapter Three

'Are you going to the wedding?' I ask Tom as I'm dipping my chip in mayonnaise.

We decided to have food and drink a few beers before going to the party.

'I'm going to the afters because Megan is head bridesmaid, so I won't be seeing much of her on the day. I don't really want to hang around with her family for the day because it would be weird, like I don't know them. Whereas at the afters, everyone will be relaxed and have a few drinks so it will be easier to mingle with them if Megan is busy with Rachel. And I'll be relaxed because I'll have a few drinks with ye before I go,' Tom says cheekily.

We go into Megan's uncle's pub or the proper name of it 'The Ringing Bell'. I asked Megan where her uncle came up with the name and she said it was from when he was younger. The bell was used for mass and when school started and finished, it had a lasting effect on him. Her uncle always finishes the story by sighing and saying 'that ringing bell'. After telling me that story, she told me to ask her uncle about the pub's name, but I decided not to because at the time he was busy talking to his regulars and I didn't want to interrupt his conversation for our amusement.

(If it were a group of girls, I would have had no problem interrupting them but they were older men who had lived through and seen a lot of wars. I am an ignorant pig in general, but I do have exceptions.)

The pub is packed with people. I find myself saying *Hello* to more people than I thought I would, but that is because a few of the men I recognise are regulars that were here the few times we were in here. I'm asking them how their wives are and even asking them about their grandchildren.

I don't know what has become of me.

Tom sees Megan. She beckons us to come over. She's standing where Tara and I talked (where I charmed her!). She's with Rachel and two men and two women I'm guessing are Rachel's fiancé and friends or relations. The two men appear similar; I wonder if are they brothers. They are both similar height about six feet with dark hair and cut the same way – the fade hairstyle with beards that have been recently trimmed which I'm sure were done today for this party. The other women are completely different; one is short with ginger curly hair and glasses while the other is tall, sallow-skinned and with dark hair.

'Hey, Tom!' She kisses Tom on the cheek. She looks at me and Conor. 'Hi, Ciaran! Hi, Conor!' and hugs us both.

Awh, I like Megan.

She turns to face the others. 'Guys, this is Max, Trish, Annie, Mike and you all know my sister Rachel.'

'Hi, guys, welcome to our pre-wedding party,' Rachel says, looking at Mike. I'm assuming he's the fiancé. 'So, Mike is my fiancé. Annie is our cousin, she's living in New York at the moment. Max is Mike's best man and Trish is Max's girlfriend.' Then Rachel turns to her companions and introduces us again even though Megan already did, but maybe she thought it would sound better coming from her. 'This is Tom, Megan's boyfriend, and this is Ciaran and Conor. They are Tom's friends.'

Yes, I prefer her re-introduction of us much better. 'Tom's friends' is who we will be for the night.

Mike doesn't seem irritated to see me. He mustn't know about mine and Tara's history. I wonder why she never told him. She never hid her feelings towards me and I'm assuming he would also show his disgust at seeing me if he knew. Maybe he's better at concealing his emotions than Tara, plus it would be a bad night to make a scene.

Mike and Trish look like a couple from one of those lame women's magazines where they are sitting on the couch together or having a fake picnic and laughing. That ridiculous *picture-perfect posed couple* all the time. Annie seems shy and reserved, she doesn't know what to think of us or maybe she hasn't the interest to engage with us.

There is plenty of chat going on about the wedding, mostly Rachel is talking and we are all listening like good pupils. I don't know what Rachel's job is, I know Megan told us but I forget now. If I had to guess, I would say a teacher.

Oh great! My glass is nearly empty, I will just drink this now and head to the bar and bring Conor.

*

'Hey, Alex, can I get two pints please, thanks.'

Conor and I headed to the bar as soon as both our glasses were empty. Tom is going to be glued to Megan and the family for the night to make a good impression. I'm so grateful to have Conor to drink with.

After I order, I turn to Conor. '*Whoooo*, that was a lot of wedding talk that I could care less about.'

'Yeah, I know. Some people are just obsessed with their weddings like there *can* be other interests in people's lives apart from some expensive party. The only people it matters to are the two people getting married, like everyone else just wants a meal and a few drinks and music. I don't get the obsession with weddings.'

'Oh, same, it's such a waste of money. I mean, what you could do with the money you save for a "glamorous" wedding, you could go on a trip around the world. But women just love the attention like it has to be their day and everyone has to be looking at the bride because it's her special day. I don't think any of the grooms care about the special day, they are just doing what the woman wants. It's all about the attention and wanting every woman to be envious of their wedding day. It's such petty crap.'

I pass Conor's beer to him. 'So, where will we go?'

As I'm saying this, I see Tara and an older woman walking our way obviously getting a drink. I'm assuming the woman is her mother. She does look a bit like Tara. She looks at me then looks away again. I don't think she expected to see me here, Megan mustn't have told her that she invited us. She definitely doesn't want to talk to me in front of her mother. But I will. Also, I want to see if her head is marked from our collision. My head was sore for four days after that. She has some power in that head.

'Hi, Tara. How are you? How's your head since our collision?' I look at her and the other woman and smile. The older woman seems to be waiting for a response and introduction.

She looks uncomfortable. 'Oh, hi, Ciaran. Yeah, my head feels fine. It was sore for a day or two but no permanent damage done.' She looks at the older woman who is smiling. 'This is my mother, Helen.'

'Hi, Helen.' I shake her hand. 'Oh, you are Mike's mother; I was just talking to him, very nice lad. I'm sure he takes after you.' I give a coy and tender smile. Flattery never hurt anyone.

I see Tara rolling her eyes. 'I'm Ciaran. I'm a friend of

Tara's.' I look at Tara and smile as I'm saying it, wondering if she will confirm this.

'Yeah, he's a friend from… college and he knows Tom who is Megan's boyfriend.'

So, they are officially an item – according to Megan, anyway. Confirmed now by Rachel and Tara. Tom will be pleased.

I smile at Helen. 'Yeah, Tom and I actually live together and so does Conor,' who kept his distance during my reintroduction and is now talking to two older men.

'The three of us met Rachel at her hen here about two months ago,' I look at Tara for confirmation. She nods. 'And Tom and Megan started going out after that so that's why we are here.' That's my way of explaining to Tara why I'm at this party without having to tell her directly.

'Wasn't that good timing for Tom and Megan,' smiles Helen.

'Yeah. It was,' I reply.

I don't bother telling her that they knew each other before the party. It would be weird talking about my friend's love life with a woman I never met before.

'What's this about the heads being sore?' Helen asks looking at Tara and then me.

Tara looks awkwardly at me. I'll take this.

'Yeah, it actually happened at the hen party. Me and Tara literally banged heads. She was coming out of the bathroom and I was going in and we just weren't expecting to see each other and *bang!* But yeah, like Tara, I had no permanent damage. That bang may have knocked some sense into me so; it didn't do me any harm.' I give a light chuckle and Tara and Helen laugh.

'Can I buy you both a drink? I can see the bride and groom

will have plenty of drink being bought for them but not the other important guests.' I give a wink to Helen and they both smile, well, Tara scoffs but I'll take it.

I buy them drinks and I get myself another pint too. Two birds and all that!

I listen attentively as Helen talks about the upcoming wedding. Even though I couldn't give a crap about how much her outfit cost and how she found it hard to find shoes to match and ended up buying them online and had to pay 30 euro extra for postage. I match her annoyance at the extra cost and her delight at the happiness of her outfit and the other obstacles they conquered for the wedding as if this was some life-changing event.

What is it really? Putting two rings on fingers and being intimate without being judged by religious people. These days, anyway, marriages don't last long. The affairs are numerous, so people are putting themselves out and spending money on an occasion that will have nothing to show but regret and resentment in years to come.

Helen is still talking about the wedding while I zoned out. She is now talking about the wedding venue. I look at Tara and I think she knows I wasn't listening to the last few parts of the conversation. She doesn't seem too bothered that I wasn't listening and her mother doesn't notice at all. I'm wondering when she will stop talking.

Thankfully, Rachel intervenes now. 'Hi, Helen. Sorry, guys, do you mind if I steal her for a moment? I just want to introduce you to my aunt and uncle.'

'Oh, yes! Great!' Helen allows Rachel to lead her to the aunt and uncle. Why the introductions couldn't wait till after we had a proper talk, I do not know.

Typical bride! When she wants something done, it has to be done her way and immediately!

Tara looks jittery. She doesn't know what to do. 'Do you want me to come too, Mom?' Tara asks, sounding hopeful.

Helen turns back and pats Tara on the shoulder, saying, 'No. You stay talking to Ciaran. Ye won't have me now going on about the wedding. Ye can finally talk about other things.'

Maybe she did pick up my disinterest in the wedding talk after all. My poker face mustn't be that good or when I zoned out, I must have actually looked like I wasn't listening. Well, if she picked up on it, she wasn't too offended by my expression because she still continued talking. Anyway, nothing I can do about it now. But why is Rachel leaving Tara alone with me? She knows Tara doesn't like me. Maybe it's because it's her night and she's not aware of any tensions between people. All tensions and dramas have to be put aside for her special night.

Bride Brain!

Helen looks at us both and leaves smiling and turns to me saying, 'It was nice meeting you, Ciaran. Thanks for the drink.'

I smile, saying, 'Yeah, you too, and no problem.'

When they are out of earshot, I say to Tara, 'Wasn't she there when you said you didn't like me?'

Tara looks at me confused and then says, 'Oh yeah. She was.'

'So, why did she intentionally leave us together or should I say why did she leave you with me?'

'I think she didn't realise it because, you know, a typical bride; they don't notice anything, only themselves. They become shallow and selfish people right up to their wedding day.' Tara rolls her eyes and takes a sip of her drink. I gulp some of my pint down too.

'So, you are having fun being part of the wedding party?' I say sarcastically.

Tara just stares at me. 'Even though I don't appreciate your sarcasm at this moment, you are right. It's a bit head wrecking. The things that bother people just baffles me and the closer they get to the wedding, the more unreasonable and crazy they get and I'm not even talking about the bride.'

I laugh and then Tara starts laughing.

She has a nice laugh.

'It'll be a great ease when it's over.' She takes another sip of her drink. 'I'm not even a big drinker, but the last few weeks I've needed one to get through all this wedding prep.'

'Good thing Rachel or your brother isn't in earshot of you saying wedding crap.'

'Huh? Wedding crap?'

'Yeah. Didn't you say wedding crap?'

'No, I said wedding prep, like "preparation". You know, preparing the wedding.'

'Oh, whoops. Heard you wrong.'

'Yeah. Jeez, I would never say *crap* in the same room as Rachel or my brother. I wouldn't be invited to the wedding.'

I take a swig of my pint. 'Yeah, I was wondering. I was thinking you are a brave woman to say that aloud. *Hmmm*. Well, I don't know what else we can talk about that's as interesting as your brother's wedding. It will be tough.'

'Yeah, it will be hard. We will have to struggle on. *Mmm*. Politics? Religion? Will we start at one of them?'

'Yes.' I answer. 'Politics sounds good to start with and then finish on religion.'

Tara grins and takes a sip of her drink – vodka and white, the one I ordered for her. I got her a double. I wonder if she knows.

She taps her nails on the glass. I'm not sure if it's nerves or agitation.

'So, how's work going? Are you busy this time of year?'

'Yeah, it's good. Yes, very busy now everyone loves a hot drink in this cold weather. I would have the same people coming into me three times a day and ordering coffees for themselves, friends and colleagues, so it's good. No matter what, people always feel like a coffee whether they are working or shopping or just passing and want to sit down before going home. I mean, I do it myself, you know, go home have a cup of tea or something and just sit in your own silence drinking.'

'Yeah.'

'Well, maybe you don't, but I do and I see others in the shop doing it too so it's not an uncommon relaxation routine.'

'Oh yeah! No! I do! Like I do exactly that but instead of tea, I might have a beer when I come home and I actually look forward to it. You know when you are halfway through the day and you think when I get home, that's what I'm going to do and I actually smile to myself when I think about it.'

'Oh yeah, where is it you work?'

'At St Hilda's primary school.'

'Primary school?'

'Yeah, I'm a teacher.'

'Oh, I thought you were an engineer. I don't know why I thought that.'

'Yeah, I started it, but I dropped out halfway through the first year. I didn't like it at all and then I worked in my uncle's garage for a year and saved and applied for teaching.'

'Yeah. One of my employees is doing Hibernia at the minute. She's nearly finished. Just one more teaching practice to go and a few more lesson plans. She was telling me about it and it just sounded like something I would never be interested in. I wouldn't have the tolerance for all the lesson plans.'

'Yeah, it is tough and just intense. If I had to do it again. I wouldn't! I do feel her pain.'

'What class do you teach?'

'I teach the third class. It's a big school so there are twenty-eight pupils in my class.'

'Wow! So, how long are you there?'

'Ah, three years now.'

'Cool! Are you permanent now or is there a process?'

'Yeah, I became permanent this year which is great. It's the first time I will have summer pay.'

'Wow, it's great to be a teacher. Paid holidays and all. What other job has that?'

'Yeah, it is great. I mean, you do get an awkward parent and awkward child to deal with.'

'Yeah, but sure that's in every job like I get the odd awkward customer, but I don't let that customer ruin my day or my work. You just think of all the nice people you have encountered. Ye get so many holidays like mid-term, Christmas and bank holidays. I have friends who are nurses and they work thirteen hours a day, and on their day off between shifts they can't even enjoy it because they are tired and getting ready for the next morning. Some of them leave at six to be there for seven to get parking. They won't start until eight. It's mad and then they have to deal with patients who hit them or are ignorant of them and family members too that are watching what they are doing. That's hard work but they never complain about it like yeah, they might say it was hard but they love their job. I would not be able to do that job. I wouldn't have the stamina or the temperament.'

'Yeah, same, I can just about do teaching and that's only six hours a day. I mean I have to read and mark tests but it doesn't take long when you put your head down and just do it and not let it build up. It is my job too so I can't complain about marking them. But like there are other teachers that don't want to do anything and the small jobs that they have to do they complain about it. We have one teacher who always tries to get out of yard duty. She says she has a headache or has to ring about her insurance or pay for something and lunchtime is the only time she can phone because they'll be closed after school. Just absolute crap, like we all know she just wants to enjoy her lunch and go on her phone or laptop to go on Instagram or do online shopping.'

'Oh my god, that is ridiculous carry on and so immature. It's her job, so she doesn't even want to do what is involved in her job. It's annoying how ye have a set pay because if it were based on the hours you work, her wage would be cut and rightly so too. We all take turns taking out the bins and nobody minds doing it, but if one person had an excuse every time it was their turn, well I would either cut their pay or fire them for not doing the menial tasks that are included with the job.'

'Yeah, I know like there's nothing we can do only talk about it. The principal said it to her. So, she did it one day but she's supposed to gather up any loose balls or jumpers the pupils may have forgotten to bring in. She just left them all outside. She claimed she forgot to do it. Then another day, she took ages gathering up the loose balls and that held the pupil class lines up. We couldn't go inside until she was ready so another teacher had to help her. It was really cold too. She knew what she was doing. She's never asked to do it now. It's just quicker and handier to not ask her.'

'That is scandalous. I don't understand that at all. That is part of her job. Some people don't even want to do their jobs any more. They want to do less. If her pay got cut, she would complain about how she works hard for her money and she doesn't deserve the pay cut. It's like priest and mass they want to say like one mass at the weekend and maybe two during the week. Like it's their job, *well*, vocation to say mass. They should be doing at least five masses a day and then visiting the sick and elderly if needed. They should be suiting the congregation they serve; instead, they want to say one mass and then have the rest of the day to themselves. These are the people who pass judgment on others for not attending mass. It's ridiculous and they get 20–50 euro for every mass. That's handy money for doing half an hour of work. They say then they are tired from it all. If there was no money going into their baskets, they might stop complaining.'

'You're not into religion and mass then.'

'No, I am. I go every week because I like the priest we go to. This mass is always packed with people but now they are not having that mass at all. They are ending it next week because "changes need to be made due to a shortage of priests". They complain about not enough young people attending mass and then the one mass that brings a good crowd they cut it.'

'Well, now that we have covered religion, shall we move on to politics now?'

She laughs and says, 'Yeah, sorry, weird how we ended up talking about that well… I vented about that.'

'Hey, when something is on your mind, it's always good to get it out and it was obviously on your mind.'

'Yeah, it was. It has really annoyed me actually. But anyway, it's like in your job; all you can do is talk about it because nothing is going to be done. In my business, if someone spilled a hot drink on themselves, they could turn around and sue me for maybe not warning them about a hot drink being hot and my insurance would pay for it. I know this for a fact because it happened to a friend of mine who owns a coffee shop. It's scandalous what is going on to decent, hard-working people. The establishments we are part of are not fair or respectable to the right people.'

'Yeah, it's all to do with money.'

'Yeah, and a lot of the time money leads to arrogance and ignorance.'

'Huh, don't know what my excuse is so.'

Tara smirks at my comment. I thought she'd like that one!

CLINK! CLINK! CLINK!

We look over and it's Rachel clinking her glass with a spoon. She must have sensed the attention was being diverted away from her and wanted it back.

'Thank you, everyone, for coming tonight to celebrate our pre-wedding nuptials gathering.' She looks at Mike and both of them smile at each other.

Urgh! Vom!

'We are grateful to all of you for coming from all parts of the world to be at our wedding and obviously very grateful to our friends and family who are near us. You all have been a great help to us with the planning of the wedding. Wedding planning as I've come to know is very stressful.' Mike nods beside Rachel and exhales. He must have felt very stressful dealing with Rachel.

'But the hard part is over and let's hope that it's smooth sailing ahead now. Thank you all again for coming and hope you enjoy the night and the wedding.'

Mike finishes, saying, 'CHEERS EVERYONE!' We all drink. He must have sensed that's what people were waiting for.

We arrive home at two in the morning. It may be early for some people, but it's late for me. All that needless wedding talk has me worn out. I'll probably be dreaming of wedding dresses tonight.

The three of us are in the sitting room eating chips. None of us are talking, the only sound we are making is the sound of us dipping our chips in salt and ketchup and tossing them into our mouths.

As I'm eating, I'm thinking of the last words I said to Tara: 'I might see you again.'

Urgh! So cheesy! And to add more cheese on the cracker, I gave her a cheeky smile and wink! *Urgh!* I feel sick, although that could be from the drink.

But I think she is succumbing to my pretend charms. Now I just have to accidentally on purpose meet her again. I do know where she works and a person always needs coffee at any time of the day.

'Why are you smiling?' asks Tom.

I'm looking at him now, confused. I was so immersed in my thoughts that I didn't realise my face was reacting to them.

'*Hmm?* Oh, I was just thinking about how good the food is after drinking,' I reply, hoping he'll believe that.

'Oh yeah, same, food is what I look forward to after drinking and water. Mike bought me a shot before we left. I had to drink a glass of water after it because I thought I was going to throw up. I can't tolerate them like I used to.' He shakes his head and puts a chip into his mouth.

'It's a sign we are getting old, Tom,' I say brazenly.

'*Haha*, yeah, older and hopefully wiser,' Tom says optimistically.

I have to respond in an ignorant and cheeky manner. '*Haha*, to quote John Wayne, that'll be the day.' The three of us chuckle in unison and continue eating.

Chapter Four

It's been a week, an appropriate time lapse. I think it's time to visit Tara's coffee shop. Friday evening is a plausible time because everyone needs a nice coffee at the end of a long hard week.

I am walking towards it now. I look in one of the big windows. It doesn't look too busy. There is the stereotypical man in the far corner on a laptop drinking coffee and three students on a lounge with three different-sized cups on their table. I keep walking past. I don't know why I'm nervous about going in. I'm only ordering a coffee.

It has an appealing look to it. The outside is painted a chestnut brown with two big windows and the entrance is at the end of the windows and on the door, there is a sign saying Welcome.

I turn back and push open the door. Tara is working, she is behind the counter with her back to me. An older woman is working with her. I wonder if she is related to Tara. She is in the middle of making coffee. There are two people ahead of me. The first person is a young woman and the next person is a young boy with headphones in his ear. The young woman takes her coffee and heads over to the students. Tara heads over to the till to ask the next person for their order. She looks up and she spots me.

She's shocked but not disgusted, nice to know a bit of my charm worked on her. It's weird not seeing those dagger eyes. Do I like it? I am not sure yet. I will admit I am a bit uncomfortable with it. She's taking the man with the headphones' order and he is undecisive, there is only so much on the menu one can order. Ridiculous, just as I am about to roll my eyes the employee interrupts my thoughts and asks, 'Hi, what can I get you?'

I smile, saying, 'Hi, can I get a cappuccino, please?'

'Yeah, small or medium or large?'

'Ahh, medium is good, thanks.' Seems reasonable to ask for medium and make out I really need the coffee. I'm also contributing to her business because I am a decent guy!

As the employee is making the coffee and the headphones guy finally makes his decision and walks off with his mocha, I think Tara waits to greet me.

'Hi, Ciaran, how are you? Passing through or did you get lost and need a coffee to find your footings again?' She smiles when she's finished. Can't decide if she's being sarcastic or generally interested.

Her employee Denise then hands me the takeaway cup and smiles. I was going to leave, but I think I'll stay now. There's no one behind me so she might join me. I could ask.

I laugh mostly because of the cheekiness in her tone.

'A bit of both, actually. It was a happy coincidence that it was your coffee shop I decided to find my footing again.'

'*Haa*, yeah, happy for you anyway.'

Her employee drops the mouth. I look at her and say, 'It's OK, we know each other, this I how we communicate with each other. I'm used to her smart remarks.'

Her employee smiles again.

'I notice there is no one behind me so do you want to join me for a quick coffee, I assume employees get a discount for their coffee.' I look at her employee and she nods and smiles, I look at Tara wondering if she got the joke or thought I was a smart ass.

She just shrugs her shoulders, pretending to be impressed by my quick wit. She looks at me takeaway cup, confused at my decision to sit down.

I look down. 'Ah yes, well, I prefer takeaway cups, stays warmer longer.'

She nods in agreement. *Hm*, that was just a chanced defence but maybe it's true.

'Come on, five mins, it can be your good deed for the day, and I am sure you will be rewarded in heaven for it.'

'Ha, I hope so, OK get a seat and I'll be there in a minute.'

YES! The plan is coming together!

She joins me with a takeaway cup too; she plans on staying longer given the cup she chose. Great!

'So, how is business?'

'Yeah, it's good, thanks. It always gets busier after five.' Why does she feel she has to defend her quiet business hours to me?

'Oh, I'm sure it is, but I always prefer coffee shops a bit quieter.' I quickly add, 'I am not trying to be condescending or ignorant, it's just what I prefer.'

She smiles, sipping her coffee. 'Yeah, me too.' *Phew!*

'So, how was your week?'

'Oh, it was fine, the usual stuff. Not too bad or destructive, had a few tantrums to deal with but they were sorted, and I am not even talking about the students.'

She bursts out laughing. Great, I made her laugh anyway. She has a nice smile and laugh. Anyway…

'How is Tom? Has his outfit been picked for the wedding and the hair booked in for the morning?'

'*Haaaaa,* he has, yeah! We are actually going tux shopping tomorrow, whatever that means; he wants to buy a tux. I said just rent one for the day but no, he wants to buy. Must be serious between him and Megan. Really out to impress her.'

'*Haaa,* yeah, that's nice though, they get on well and look nice together. I hope he didn't tell Megan a week before the wedding that he's going tux shopping.'

Ah, I am a bit flustered. '*Ah*, I don't know, maybe I let the cat out of the bag. Oops, please don't tell her, this is an opportunity to paint me in a bad light now. Damn!'

She's looking as if she is contemplating causing trouble. Crap! Me and my big mouth.

'No, I won't say anything, he's earlier than most men. Usually, it's the day before.'

'*Phew,* thanks, don't think I would see next week if he knew Megan was told. He *is* mad about her, so he would definitely kill me if I annoyed her.'

'No, I won't say anything, might not even see her. Rachel will certainly keep her busy.'

We both sip her coffee.

'So, how is your brother, is he nervous?'

Tara folds her lips in indicating there are nerves but she probably won't let him down by admitting it.

'Yeah, he is nervous.'

What? I am staring at her now, shocked she was so honest.

'Like not nervous about marrying Rachel, but he's not one for attention being on him. He's a plumber; if he was a teacher or solicitor, he would be used to talking and people paying attention to him, so I think the speech and photos are what he's nervous about.'

'Oh right.'

'Yeah, like he's not shy but comfortable in small surroundings, those jobs are linked with a bit of arrogance in people, you are well suited to it.' She smirks as she's sipping her coffee.

Oh, what a cheeky bitch.

'Oh yes, sure as you know from early experience that my arrogance is trailing after me, I am sure I can spare some to give your brother if he would like my sort of arrogance for the day?'

She laughs at this; I am doing well.

'I'll ask him and let you know! Tom is all right getting there, then there's a few roundabouts and two side roads.'

'Yeah, he'll be fine, I'm dropping him off and collecting him, just handier 'cos I think all the bridesmaids are sharing two rooms and the hotel was full by the time he and Megan started dating. Think he's just bothered about walking into the venue on his own, but a few drinks and he'll be fine.'

Tara just looks away. I wonder did she just zone me out, don't think I was talking crap but maybe she doesn't care about the job situation.

She turns to me then and says, 'Well, seeing as though you are driving him, why don't the two of ye come in, it's the afters so… you may as well, and Tom will be at ease if he can't find Megan or if she's busy.'

'Do you know I would normally put on "oh no, it's fine" and wave my hand away at you, but I think that would be a big help for Tom. He was dreading it, I felt sorry for him that's why I offered to drive him.'

'Well, that's settled then.' She takes a final gulp of her cup and stands up. 'I'll see the two of ye next Saturday, I better get back to work; otherwise, the boss will dock my wages.' She gives a sarcastic smile.

'Yeah, I better head off too.' She takes both our cups and smiles finishing up, saying, 'Bye.'

I'll get the last word in now, 'Yeah, bye, Tara, and thanks.'

'No problem.'

Fine, she can have the last word. Because I will have the last laugh!

Chapter Five

'Tom, you look fine.'

Tom is fixing his tie in the mirror in the hall, and he turns to me and says, 'Fine? I look fine? I don't want to look fine.'

I roll my eyes. '*Argh!* Right, what way do you want to look, and I will say it. Handsome? Pretty? Gorgeous, any of those?'

'*Urgh!* You are so annoying; I need to look sophisticated and smart and dapper and a man her family would love to see more of.'

'Ooohhh, right well, that's it. Well, you look all those things, it's only been a few months, Tom, jeez relax, take deep breaths, follow my lead. In through your nose and out through the mouth.'

'You're an asshole.' Tom fixes his tie again.

'Argh! If you fix that tie again, I will rip it off you and throw it in the bin, now come on.'

'Oooh, now who's in a hurry to get there? Excited about seeing Tara, are we?'

'NO, just want to go when I am ready and not be waiting around.'

'Yeah, sure, whatever you say.' He gives me a cheeky smile. If he only knew what my plan with Tara is, but the less he knows, the better the plan will work. He puts on his jacket and takes one more look in the mirror.

'Right, I am ready. Let's go.'

As we turn into a gateway for the hotel, we both have the same expression on our faces which is amazed, both mouths open. The grounds are massive, there is greenery on either side of the laneway. The hotel is four storeys high and the fountain at the front of the hotel is the size of a football pitch. Why would you need such a big fountain?

We are greeted with a valet as we drive beside the hotel. Good thing I got the car washed; otherwise, it would be embarrassing, more so for Tom than me. The soon-to-be in-laws probably would not be impressed with him driving in with a dirty car.

We are not used to this kind of treatment and the valet worker I'm sure knows we are not from high society families. He just stands and smiles, waiting for us to get out of the car. As we get out, he walks over and greets us while taking the keys. Tom and I smile, we are in such shock I don't think we spoke to the valet driver. Anyway, time to go in.

The front entrance has a red carpet all along the lobby and there are people wandering in and out of doors. There's laughter coming from one door and loud music from another. We see a sign saying Rachel and Mike's wedding. Of course, Rachel's name would be first or maybe that's the norm. Something I'll never know about. Never plan to anyway.

We walk in and it is packed with people, the dance floor is packed with people from all different ages. I spot the bride and groom on the dancefloor. Great, we missed the first dance; I hate all that staring and pretending to be so in awe of the bride and groom. I also see Tara on the dancefloor, she's dancing with a man who looks in his late 50s or 60s. Must be her uncle. They all look like they are having a good time and enjoying the drink that seems to be on all the tables. I look at Tom, I know who he's looking for, but I can't spot Megan either. I would assume she's with the bride but Rachel is on the dancefloor.

'Hey, guys, how are ye? Are ye here long?'

We both turn and yes it's Megan. Tom greets her with a hug and kiss on the cheek, probably has to appear to be a respectable boyfriend.

She hugs me too.

'Hi, Megan. Yeah, we just came in here; a very fancy place. A valet at the door so he took the car, not used to that kind of treatment.'

Megan appears confused, did I stutter?

'Ah, what are you talking about? A valet? There's no valet parking here.

OK, now I am confused. 'Ah, what, are you sure? He was in a suit with the hotel logo on his jacket and he took the car. Seemed to know what he was doing.'

'No, no one mentioned a valet parking attendant.'

I look at Tom and he looks at me we are about to start running out when Megan starts laughing.

'I'm only joking. Yes, there is valet parking. My uncle said that to my cousin's boyfriend earlier and he ran out before my uncle could tell him he was joking. Oh god, he came back in such a state he had to sit down 'cos he got such a fright. He drives a Jaguar so that would be expensive for the car to get stolen. We were all in stitches laughing. *Awh*, the poor man. My cousin just went to him, "welcome to the family!" He eased up a bit later. It was very funny. If you see my uncle, he'll probably tell you that story, he's very proud of it.'

'Oh, *phew*, not that I drive a Jaguar but still wouldn't like the old girl stolen.'

Megan exhales. 'Oh, what is with men calling their car a her or she? I don't get it. If it drives, it's a car.'

'Yeah, you just don't get it, Megan. Treat a car right and she is your girl. You know how nice a man is by the way he treats his car, just remember that. I think Tom treats his car well. Right, Tom?'

We both look at Tom; my expression is more amused than Megan's.

'Yeah, I treat my car nice.' He's awkward about these things. Megan looks at us both and changes the subject.

'Anyway, you both look nice. Come on, we'll go to the bar.'

'OK, but I am driving so I can't drink too much, just a few pints, don't want to be too drunk driving.'

Tom laughs and Megan looks weary.

'Megan, I am joking. I'll only drink three. Joking again. No, I'll have one and that's my limit.'

It will be out of my system in a few dances. I nod over towards the dancefloor and notice one of the groomsmen doing the robot. Oh, I can't *not* look at it.

'Well, you can play it by ear because there are two rooms available now 'cos two of Rachel's work friends couldn't make it. They are booked anyway so see how you feel. You might feel like eight pints as the night goes on.'

She's talking to me, but I feel it's more for Tom's benefit. She's letting him know they can literally get a room.

'Yeah, we'll see. Thanks, Megan.'

The three of us stand just off from the bar enjoying drinks and conversation when Rachel beckons Megan over to help with her dress for the bathroom.

'Sorry, guys, duty calls. I'll be back in a few minutes, take a seat somewhere if ye want. Think some finger food will be coming out in a few minutes and if ye feel like going wild, ye should go out on the dancefloor. Ye know nearly all the women on it already from the hen party. All big fans of the two of ye.'

I scoff, saying, 'You are not serious.'

'I am deadly serious, they all had great fun with ye at the hen party and the family party too.'

She's either a very good liar or being genuine. She's looking at both of us now, wondering why we don't believe her.

'I thought with the whole Tara business, they would particularly hate me and—'

Tom interrupts, 'Yeah and me because I am associated with him.'

I look at Tom. 'Thanks, Tom.'

He looks at me, smiling, 'Well, you know what I mean, I am good friends with you, naturally I'd stick up for you.'

'Thanks, mate,' I say, feeling humbled.

Megan interrupts our bro moment. 'Looks like ye need to get a room, don't let me interrupt.'

We both look at her, we need to defend our "broment". I grunt purposely, pretending to wipe away tears 'Sorry, Megan, we just get touching moments like this, and I just feel so emotional right now. Think I need a tissue. Tom, you normally keep one in your pocket for me.'

Tom taps his jacket pocket. 'Sorry, mate, it's in my other jacket.' We both start laughing.

'Right, I'll let this touching moment continue 'cos Rachel is giving me the eye, see ye in a while.'

We both pretend to be blubbering as she leaves us.

'Ah that was fun, so will you stay the night?'

'Will you?'

'Well, I suppose I'll finish this,' I say, holding up my pint, 'and if I feel I want another and another, then I might take the room.'

'Yeah, sure, we'll play it by ear, I suppose.'

Well, you'll probably be sharing a room and it won't be with me, but I can always swap and go in with one of the bridesmaids.' I put my hand on his shoulder. 'I do love you, Tom, but I just prefer to share my bed with a woman.'

'Yeah, I kind of feel the same way too, so if it works out that way, then I am going to share with Megan.'

'Cheers to that.'

'Cheers.' We both clink our pints and laugh.

I look toward the dancefloor and Tara is gone; I spot her talking to her mother. Great, her mother loves me, well, likes me anyway. She smiled a lot when we talked so I'll settle for that. Just can't remember her mother's name, DAMN. They are both walking over this way. *CRAP! What is her name?*

They are both coming towards me and Tom, they spot us and smile, and we smile back. While keeping the smile on my face, I discreetly ask Tom what Tara's mother's name is, but he doesn't know. Feck him anyway.

'Oh, Helen, you look lovely.' They both turn slightly, and some other woman is talking to them. *Thank you, random woman, now I know her name; Helen.* I'll get points for remembering her name, they have to be impressed with my good memory and it will show I took an interest in our last meet.

I suppose we should stay as we are because they will be coming over to us and it would appear rude if we walked off. No matter what excuse we might give them later, it would still be seen as rude.

They finish their conversation and are now walking towards us.

I'll greet them first. 'Hi, Helen and Tara. How ae ye this evening? You both look absolutely stunning. I would put you both as sisters of the groom.' I am such a flatterer.

'Oh, you flatterer,' Helen says. 'Thank you, how very kind of you. I'm sorry I have forgotten your name.'

'Oh, it's fine, I—'

Tara interjects, 'This is Ciaran and Tom. Tom is seeing Megan and I asked Ciaran to come because Tom would be on his own while Megan performs her bridesmaid duties.'

She's going to a lot of trouble to explain the reason I am here.

'Oh, it's nice you two kept in contact with one another after the party,' Helen says curiously.

I look at Tara and give her a look that indicates I'll take this, Tara.

'Well, I popped into her café, and we got talking about the wedding, so Tara kindly asked for my assistance for Tom. She felt bad knowing he would be on his own so, of course, being the gentleman I am, I accepted her request so here we are now at this fabulous event, enjoying the drinks and, of course, the company.'

No surprise, Tara rolls her eyes and Helen is ecstatic with the continued flattery I give her.

'Mum.' I look and see Mike coming over. 'Hi, everyone, hope you are enjoying the night.' He turns to his mother. 'Mum, where did you put the bag of cards? I just got two more.'

Helen looks at us all and rolls her eyes and gasps, 'I'll get it.'

Mike holds his hand up. 'No, it's fine, Mum, stay talking. I'll get it if you tell me where it is.'

'No, because I can't quite remember where I put it, so I'll look, give me those and off you go. Nice seeing you two again.' Helen follows Mike towards one of the tables.

So now, it's the three of us and this is the time Tom decides to leave to use the bathroom. Traitor.

So now, it's me and Tara.

'So, are ye here long?'

'No, we got here about ten minutes ago. We were talking to Megan for a while but then she had to go help Rachel with her dress.'

'Oh right, ye missed the first dance so lucky you.'

'Oh yeah, what was their song?'

Tara scoffs at this question, this will be interesting. '"Queen of My Heart" by Westlife. Can't believe they chose that song, it's so cheesy.'

'Is she a fan of Westlife?'

'*Ah,* not a fan, but she likes their earlier songs, she said she had good memories when she was younger that were associated with their songs so that's why she wanted one of their songs. Then I think my brother came back from work humming that song and she thought it was a sign to pick that song, so yeah, that's the reason they, well, she picked it.'

'Sorry I missed it now, I would have liked to see your face while dancing to that song. Who was your dance partner?'

'*Ah.*' She turns towards the dancefloor. 'Nick, the guy there dancing with my aunt.'

'Oh yeah, he's a good mover.'

'Yeah, he is and his wife is dancing with Mike.'

'Ah, so you can't go there so.'

'What?' She looks confused.

'You know, the bridesmaid normally cops with one of the groomsmen.'

'Oh *haaa*, yeah, they are all married so NO.'

'Are the wives all here?' I ask mischievously.

'Yeah, they are, and they are watching their men like

hounds.'

'Oh, right, so the cliché won't happen at this wedding.'

'No, not at this one, but I think one of the bridesmaids will cop off with one of the men that came to the afters.'

I feel it, my mouth just dropped.

'Relax, I'm talking about Megan and Tom.'

'Oh yes.' Right, time to change the subject. I look at the dancefloor. 'Looks like your mother found where she kept the cards.'

Tara turns and sees Helen dancing with her husband.

Tara turns back to me and says, 'You definitely didn't know my mother's name, you asked Tom before we talked to the two of you, didn't you?'

'You noticed that?'

Tara nods.

'I did, but he didn't know so I was panicking; it was a relief when another person said her name before you both came over to us.'

'I know, I cursed Margaret for saying my mother's name because I was curious to see if you remembered it.'

'Yeah, must buy this Margaret a drink for saving me from embarrassment.' I look around to see if I can spot her anywhere.

'Yeah, she's recently divorced so I think if you put on the same flattery show as you did for my mother, she'll be your big fan for the night.'

'*Ah*, that flattery was saved just for your mother.'

We both share a laugh and then there's a pause between us.

Suppose, I'll start a new conversation. I grunt. 'So, how was the meal?' Yeah, not a great change of topic but it was the first that came to mind when I saw the finger food coming out.

'Yeah, it was nice, had salmon because I think it's a safer

option. There was also beef but sometimes it's not cooked fully so ends up being very chewy.'

'Yeah, I probably would have chosen the salmon too, I like my meat well done, crumples in your mouth.'

'Yeah, me too.'

This just got weirdly intimate and it's meat we are talking about.

'I was just going to get a drink before the food came out and now it's out, what is it you are drinking?'

'Ah, Heineken, hey stop. Tara, I'll get these. Here, you hold this' – I give her my pint – 'and I'll go to the bar. Actually, where are ye sitting and I'll bring them down.'

'Yeah, that's handier, Thanks, yeah just sitting… do you see that table where the red coat is? Well, I'm just behind that table.'

'OK, grand, I'll see you in a minute.'

Tara smiles. 'Great. Thanks.' I thought I did well to get one smile from her while in my company but there must have been about ten now. She succumbed to my charm quickly.

After a long minute, I finally get the two drinks. Should I have bought one for her mother? Oh well, I only have two hands so just have to leave it at the two. Anyway, I must get points from Helen for buying her daughter a drink.

I head over to the table and there's a free seat beside Tara. I wonder if it's that a happy coincidence or did she save me a seat. There is also another woman and two men.

'Now finally got the drinks.'

Tara smiles again. 'Oh thanks, Ciaran. Ciaran, this is my cousin Melanie. She's living in England. And Sam is our brother and Will is another cousin of ours. So, you know nearly all the family now.'

Before anyone can think I am her boyfriend, she continues

by saying, 'This is Ciaran, he is a friend of Megan's boyfriend.'

I just realised I haven't seen Tom since he left for the bathroom. He's probably fine but Tara notices me looking around.

'Are you all right?'

'Yeah, I just realised I haven't seen Tom since he went to the bathroom.'

'Oh, I am sure he met Megan coming out with Rachel and he's with her.'

'Yeah, he's not lost anyway or looking for me! Probably went and got a room.'

'Oh, hopefully, it's not in our room!'

I look at her quizzically.

'Me and Megan are sharing a room.'

'Oh, right well, hopefully, it's one of the spare rooms that are free.'

'Oh, there are free rooms?'

'Yeah, something like two of Rachel's work friends couldn't make it so she told us there were two spare rooms if we wanted one.'

'Right, did ye take one?'

'Well, I said we'd see how we feel. But I also said I was only having one pint, and this is my second so… might have to book the room.' I purse my lips with a smile and take a sip of my pint.

Tara's reaction is neutral. Let's see where the night takes us, I'll probably end up passed-out in a room.

The drinks are flowing I have had about six drinks thanks to Tara's cousins and Tara herself buying a round of drink (I was about to go to the bar when Tara held me down and said it was her turn). No one has left the table in well over an hour except when they bought drinks.

A song comes on that Melanie loves and she drags Tara out on the dancefloor, she's gesturing to the three of us to join them. We all give in and head towards the dancefloor. I then see Tom walking over, so I give a sign that I'm going to talk to Tom. Tara nods and must be explaining it to Melanie because Melanie doesn't push for me to join.

'Hey, thanks for ditching me, you were awhile in the bathroom. Was there a queue or had you a sick stomach?'

Tom picks up on my sarcasm immediately.

'*Hahaa*, so funny. No, I really did go to the bathroom but I met Megan and Rachel coming out, so Rachel said Megan is off-duty for a while so may as well spend time with her boyfriend. So, we went out to the bar, and she booked a room for me and you.' He gestures his hands between the two of us.

'More like you and her.'

Tom gives a grimacing look. 'Well, I don't know; you may get very drunk and vomit then the room will be all yours and I'll have to bunk in with Megan and another bridesmaid.'

'No, I have had my fill of pints so I'm happy not to drink any more. *Ah*, ya know, Megan is sharing with Tara.'

'What, no? really? She never said, well that room has two beds and the room just booked has a double bed, so Tara's room might be a better option for a good sleep.'

'Yeah, yeah, yeah, cut your fake consideration. If I end up in that room, I don't mind. I'll put my head anywhere for the night.'

I look over at the dancefloor and see Tara dancing with someone I haven't noticed tonight. I dare say he is more attractive than me. She is laughing and smiling a lot with him. My body wants to go over there right away, but my head is telling me to sit down with Tom. Guess I'll listen to my head.

As Tom and I sit down, he asks, 'So, how was it with Tara?'

'Yeah, it was fine, I mean I'm talking to her and her cousins most of the time. Melanie encouraged us all to the dancefloor, but I saw you just in time to prevent me from showing them up with my spectacular moves.'

'The two of you are getting on grand considering you both don't like one another.'

'I never said I didn't like her, I said she didn't like me.'

'*Oooooh*, are we trying to win her approval?'

'No, just no harm in trying to prove her wrong.'

Tom raises his eyebrows up and down as he takes a gulp of his drink.

We are beckoned over by Melanie to join them on the dancefloor. Suppose we better be good guests and join them. The few drinks I had help me dance like I don't care and put on a pretence that I am a great dancer. We are on the dancefloor for what feels like five minutes, but it it's actually thirty and the DJ is finishing his set and announces his last song, which is Take That's "Never Forget". It gets everyone up to join in the chorus for putting the hands up to clap.

We go back to our table and the conversation is flowing; everyone is talking and listening to other topics around the table. I am not ready for the night to end, and it appears the feeling is mutual around the table. We all head to the residents' bar, and as me and Tom are residents now, we follow everyone out.

Megan joins the group so that's who Tom will be beside for the rest of the night. They'll probably go off without telling anyone, but who will tell Tara who her new bunk buddy will be? Or has she assumed it will be me and is accepting it?

After two hours of conversation and drinking, my eyes start to feel heavy, I would happily sleep on this seat right now. I assumed Tom left, but I get a tap on the shoulder and it's Tom, thankfully, and he's holding a room card.

'Hey, Ciaran, Megan said to give you her room key. We're going to head up now and you looked wrecked, *ah*, also she told Tara, so she doesn't mind.'

My eyes feel like they are going to fall in, so I happily take the key and follow them up. There is no one in the room when I open the door, which is great. No need for conversation, just need to find the bed and I am gone. I don't know where Tara went but right now, I like being on my own.

I wake slightly to the sound of a thump on the floor. My head is banging so I switch on the light in a sleepy haze.

Tara is taking her shoes off on the floor.

'Sorry, did I wake you? I was trying to come in easy and keep the light off, but I forgot my suitcase was at the end of my bed and tripped so decided while I'm down here I'll take off my shoes. Turn off the light again 'cos I'm just going straight to bed.'

'No, it's OK, my head is killing me anyway, so I won't be sleeping for a while.' I pull back the covers and go to the bathroom for water.

'I have paracetamol in my suitcase if you want to take one before you go to sleep.'

I'm gulping down water and pouring more water into the glass when I come out to the room and answer her. 'Yeah, that would be great. Thanks.'

She roots in her suitcase for the tablets, she's bending, and it looks uncomfortable while wearing that dress.

'You are surely not going to sleep in that?'

She looks down at her dress. 'Ah well, I would've because it's hard to unzip but since you are awake, maybe you could unzip me? Oh, and here's your paracetamol.' I go to grab the box, but she takes back her hand. 'Tablets for zip, please.'

I huff, 'Fine, turn around.'

She turns obediently. I never noticed all these buttons. 'Do I have to unbutton all these?'

She turns her head. 'What? Oh no, there's a zip there, just pull the buttons aside.'

'Oh yes, *phew*, I'd be here all night.' Tara laughs.

'Yeah, I would be probably asleep while you were doing it.'

I scoff, this may have been a tender moment between us, only my head is killing me to take it in, so I unzip her, swallow two tablets and lie back in bed as she walks into the bathroom to change.

'So, did you enjoy the night?' Tara asks from the bathroom.

I pull my head up. 'Yeah, it was a fun night, more fun than I thought it would be.' Oops, maybe shouldn't have said that. Damn this headache.

Tara comes out from the bathroom wearing an I shot JR t-shirt and shorts. I laugh saying 'Nice T-shirt' and I put my head back on the pillow.

'Oh, Thanks, it's a great T-shirt. You get it, right?'

I raise my head. 'Yeah, I get it, Father Ted.'

'Yeah.' She seems pleased.

I lie back down and say, 'All you're missing is the unibrow and shotgun.'

I hear Tara pull back the covers and lie in bed. 'So more fun than you expected, that's good.'

'Yeah, well, you know what I mean. I didn't know anyone so wasn't sure if I would be sitting at the bar on my own all night waiting for Tom.'

'Right, yeah, you might have ended up sitting on the bar waiting, but you certainly would not be alone.'

I sit up, curious by her statement. 'What do you mean?'

She looks over at me. 'I mean, I'm sure one or two women would see you on your own and feel sorry for you and it would lead to an eventful night for you.'

I look at her with my mouth open; she's not wrong, I would probably find a desperate woman to chat up to pass the time. 'You know I would like to say you would be wrong, but actually, that would sound about right.'

She faces forward, I'm sure delighted with herself for knowing me so well. I could leave it there and end the night on a high for her and me for leaving her that way, but I am curious what else she might say so I follow on with 'I don't see anything wrong with women finding me attractive and me flattering them with my charm. Isn't that the way it's supposed to be, a charming man making a woman feel good about themselves, buy them a few drinks and finishing the night with a bit of fun? Maybe you are a prude for that kind of entertainment.' I refrain from smiling.

Tara looks over at me again. 'I am not a prude; I just don't see the need in men being so arrogant about pulling a woman and then making them feel like crap for their own amusement. I know women can be just as slutty as men, but women don't brag about their behaviour whereas men do. Women are more conservative and jovial about their experience with handsome men.'

'Suppose you can't change generations of men behaving that way, so why start now?' I keep eye contact with her.

'Yeah, just have to find the ones who aren't arrogant and ignorant.' She's thinking and continues, 'Forget it, I'll be on my own forever. I can live with that.' She lies on the bed and turns over.

'You never know, Tara; if you are persistent enough, you might change one man's arrogance and ignorance.'

Tara turns over to face me and puffs the air. 'Yeah, I'm sure he'll come into the coffee shop and I'll just get a feeling I have to change him.'

'You never know, stranger things have happened. Anyway, I'm going to bed, my headache has finally eased. Night.' I turn over.

'Yeah, night, Ciaran.'

Next move, go to her coffee shop again.

Chapter Six

The weekend can now commence. Think I need a coffee, it is a good reason to pop by a certain coffee shop. I didn't want to go too soon in case I appeared desperate. The next morning after the wedding was pleasant. I was awake before Tara so I had a shower to remove the last of the alcohol and to wake myself up because I thought if I had laid down again, I would fall asleep for the day. I didn't think my drooling would be an appealing display when Tara woke up.

Tara was awake and taking pins out of her hair when I came out of the bathroom. It wasn't the typical image of me wearing a towel and her admiring my toned stomach. I had already put on my shirt and pants because I thought it would be weird if she woke while I was in the middle of dressing. We exchanged pleasantries, letting each of us know how we slept. Tara then went to shower, she wanted to wash all the hairspray out of her hair. I decided to wait for her before heading down for breakfast, she also was dressed when she exited the bathroom. We both headed down straight away. We saw Tom and Megan, so we sat with them during breakfast. The same pleasantries were exchanged about our sleep as we ate. Tom and I chatted to the wedding party for about an hour after breakfast (then as everything we had was in our pockets), we left.

I wasn't sure if Megan and Tom were fishing for details until Tom and I were in the car, and he asked me what really happened between me and Tara. I let him know that I was a pure gentleman and that he had nothing to worry about. No arguments or sides would not need to be taken between Megan and Tom regarding me and Tara.

When I said that, he really thought something happened. I had to keep assuring him and repeating the story of how we both passed out when we lay in our beds. There was no time for arguing or foreplay of any kind. Tom then decided to brag about the great time he and Megan had in their room, and he was grateful that I had the few drinks.

Tara's coffee shop is very busy, there are eight people ahead of me in the line. Don't think Tara will have time to look at me, never mind talk to me. By the looks of it, I will also be sitting either near a couple who seem to be arguing quietly or the three teenagers who are on their phones. Finally, it is my turn and it's Tara that is serving me.

I smile at her, and she smiles back. 'Hey, Tara, how are you?'

'Hi, Ciaran. Yeah, good, thanks. Very busy today, what can I get you?'

'Coffee, black, thanks,' I say.

'Is it for sit down or takeaway?'

'*Ah*, sit down, thanks.'

She turns to make the coffee, and continues the conversation, 'So, how have you been since the wedding?'

'*Hmm?* Oh, fine yeah, it was a good wedding, but I was so tired for about two days after it. How about you?'

She hands me my coffee. 'Yeah, I was tired too after the wedding. We stayed at the bar for the entire day. I could not look at a drink for like two weeks. I met a friend a week after the wedding and all I could drink was water. She thought I was pregnant.' Tara laughs at that ridiculous notion.

I acknowledge her laugh with a laugh too. I'm conscious of the people behind me so I take the cup and say thanks to Tara. I turn to head to the table I prebooked in my mind when I walked in. The teenagers have gone, and it seems they brought their cups with them or binned them because Tara and her employees were too busy to leave the counter. Nice to see teenagers helping in their way. I grab a paper nearby; I really don't care about the news, but I need to look busy reading it while secretly watching Tara work and waiting to see if she will come to chat if the place gets quiet.

I take my time going through it, really, I'm looking at the photos. Every time I look up at Tara, she is smiling at the customers, engaging in conversation with them while conversing with her employees. The atmosphere feels very friendly and platonic. I'm wondering if she is always like this or secretly hiding what she thinks of some people with a more friendly smile. One cannot possibly like everyone.

I slyly glance at my watch, I am here nearly forty minutes, and the place hasn't quietened yet. I can't stay any longer with the same cup so I will either have to buy another or leave. I feel a presence near my table and a cup is placed on it.

'Here, I thought you might want another cup, that one has to be cold now.' I look up and it's Tara's smiling face. I must look confused because she follows with 'It's on the house, by the way.'

'Thanks, Tara, I'll leave a generous tip when I leave.'

She waves her hands away. 'No need.' She lowers her head down and speaks softly, 'Have you noticed anything?' She moves her head around the coffee shop to instruct me to do the same.

I look around and look at Tara. 'The same women are still here.' I answer softly. 'Why?'

She smiles. 'I think you have given them something to stick around for.'

'I don't get it.'

She widens her eyes and says low again, 'Eye candy, they have bought at least two cups of coffee since you sat down, so thanks, more business. Enjoy your coffee. Do you want a muffin or…?'

'Oh no, I'm fine, thanks.'

'No problem.'

Weird to be getting a free drink instead of buying one, it is only coffee but better than nothing. I sip my coffee and try to subtlety study my surroundings. The couple who were arguing have gone.

Two women are reading and the other three give glances my way while looking at their phones. I'm wondering will any one of them be brave enough to come sit at my table or by glancing at me, they are letting me know that they would be open to me joining any one of them. Well, if it were any other place, there would be one, maybe two, lucky contenders, but seeing as though I have to put on this nice guy persona, I will have to stay at my table and pretend my own ignorance to the plenty of variety I could have my pick of tonight.

I get a message from my brother Gary informing me that he's coming over the next weekend from London for his friend's stag. He wants to organise dinner and drinks with me and an old friend of his on the Friday before the stag. I am messaging him back and forth about his plans when I feel another presence approaching my table. I'm going to have to let one of the women down easily now. But when I look up, it's Tara. She places a cup of tea and a plate with two cookies on the table.

I drop my phone immediately to let her think I would drop anything for her time.

'Hey, sorry, can I join you?'

'Yeah, of course.'

'The place has finally quietened down now, so I have time to chat. How have you been since I saw you last?' She smiles and offers me the plate to take a cookie.

I take one. 'Thanks. Yeah, I have been fine, all quiet really.' My phone buzzes. 'Sorry, it's my brother, he's coming for a stag next weekend and wants to meet up.' I had to tell her in case she thinks it's a woman and then my plan would disintegrate.

I quickly write *'I'll ring you in an hour for a chat, I'm busy at the minute.'*

He replies instantly with a thumbs-up emoji. Now back to my chat with Tara.

'So how has everyone been since the wedding?'

Tara finishes eating her cookie before she answers. 'Yeah, good, Mike and Rachel are still on their honeymoon. They went two weeks after their wedding, on a cruise for ten days so they are coming back tomorrow, I think. Then they'll probably start having children as soon as possible. Rachel is a woman who has a plan; house, marriage and children.' She places her hands in a juxtaposed position as she states the stages.

I take another sip of my coffee and I think it will be my last sip because it's lukewarm. 'I suppose Mike is one of those who is happy to go with the plan to make Rachel happy.'

'Yeah, more or less. They have been together eight years, so I think they discussed her plan many times and if he hasn't jumped ship before now, well, I don't think he will anytime soon, but you never know. Plenty of people I went to school with and neighbours split. I thought those couples would be together forever, but things change, like cheating, or they outgrew one another or a few domestic issues so you really never know. But I hope for Mike's sake that it lasts. I think he would take it bad if they broke up.'

'What? He really relies on Rachel?'

'Yeah, he does,' Tara says as she takes a sip of her tea. I smile in recognition.

I look around. 'Wow, the place has really cleared in the last few minutes.'

'Yeah, think your fanbase saw me sit down so they thought you'd be too busy to flatter them. Probably all outside waiting.'

'I'll wait for the queue to get a bit longer before I go out. It's good to keep them waiting, keeps them all keen.'

'Yeah, good thinking.'

Hmm, thought she would roll her eyes at my smugness. She might be starting to like me.

'Probably the other side of the door is your fanbase.'

She looks shocked and confused. 'What? I don't have a fanbase.'

'You definitely do,'

'No, I don't. Where is my fanbase?' She gestures around the café.

'I saw you talking to all your customers and smiling. They all leave with their coffees or whatever they order, and they have smiles on their faces. It's as if you lift them up after their day. I saw a few coming in annoyed and then turning from the counter with a smile.'

She presses her lips together and pulls her head back. 'What? Really?'

'Yeah, how do you not notice?'

'I don't know, I suppose I don't really look at the door. I look at the counter and if no one is there, I'm doing something else.' She looks pleased with my comment. I wasn't trying to flatter her; it is true the way people changed their features after their order. I was sitting for forty minutes and couldn't endure looking at the paper any longer, so I had to people-watch for my own amusement and to pass the time.

We talk for another half an hour about her café, my job, our interests and even things like what sport we love and hate the most. One of her employees named Jen (her name badge is still on her blouse) walks over and says goodnight to us both. She gives Tara the eyes to indicate for her to enjoy the night. She wasn't very subtle.

She looks at her watch. 'Oh my God, is that the time? I better clean up.' She gets up, but I stop her, saying, '*Ah,* I think Jen already did that. Look!'

She looks at the counter and around the café. 'Oh wow, I didn't even notice. Must thank her tomorrow. She didn't have to do that.'

'See, blind to your own ignorance. She did it because you are a nice boss and she wanted you to sit for a while.' We both smile at one another, and I think it is time for me to go. 'Thanks for the free coffee, I better head off.' I stand to get my jacket behind my chair, take the two cups and leave them on the counter.

'Oh, there's no need, Ciaran, but thanks.' She takes the plate from the table, places it in the sink, grabs the two cups and does the same with them. I don't think it would be wise to leave a tip so I say instead, 'This was nice.'

She turns from the sink and faces me. 'Yeah, it was. Wow, can't believe how the evening flew.'

'Yeah, I know.' OK, here it goes. '*Ah,* I know you are

probably busy with the café and everything, but if you are free for an evening, I would like to repay you for the hospitality. You know free coffee and cookie. I could reciprocate with one free meal?'

She's thinking. '*Ah*, yeah, that would be nice. *Ah*, I'll just check when I'm off. It's written in the calendar.' She turns to look at a calendar hanging near the sink.

'OK, I am off Wednesday evening. Does that suit?'

'Yeah, that suits. *Ah*, should I meet you there or here or…?'

'No, you can pick the place and I will meet you. If that's OK?'

'Yeah, that's fine. OK, I will think of a place, book it and let you know. Can you give me your number?'

'Yes, I can.' She calls out her digits.

'OK, cool, I will let you know. Night and thanks.' I put on my jacket and walk towards the door.

'Yeah, night, Ciaran, safe home.' She follows me out, waves goodbye and locks the door.

Chapter Seven

'Great. Thanks.' That's the restaurant booked. I'm about to text Tara and give her the details but maybe ringing her would be more chivalry. She picks up on the fifth ring.

'Hello?'

'Hi, Tara.'

'Hi, Ciaran, how are you?'

'Good, thanks, I'm just letting you know that I booked a restaurant for Wednesday night at half seven. Does that time suit?'

'Yeah, it suits, where is it?'

'Oh, sorry yeah, it's the Blue Biscuit. Were you ever there before?'

'No, I haven't. I've never heard of it to be honest.'

'Yeah, I never heard of it either, it was Tom who told me about it. He went two or three times to it and said they do lovely food. Well, I'm hoping he's telling me the truth, he's not really one to mess with me. It's usually the other way around unless this is a revenge ploy, *ha-ha*. Anyway, if the food isn't nice, we can always go to yours for a coffee... I mean your coffee shop, not your place.'

'Don't worry, I knew what you meant. Yeah, that's fine, Ciaran, I'll see you Wednesday at half seven.'

'See you then, Tara. Bye.' *I hope Tom isn't messing with my head.*

I arrive at the restaurant at exactly half seven. I didn't want to arrive too early and appear eager; also, if I showed up late, it would appear that I didn't take this seriously or care. So, I thought on time would appear I'm enthused about the date and relaxed. The maitre d shows me to the table and I am just about to sit down when I see Tara waiting at the door. I like that she's a punctual person and not having me wait a half hour while she does her make-up and hair. It either means she doesn't care about the date or she's an easy-going person and doesn't take herself seriously or put pressure on herself to look perfect like a lot of women.

She walks over with a smile on her face, and I smile back.

'Hi, Ciaran, are you long here?' She looks at her watch. 'Just two minutes late, not too bad.'

'Yeah, I have just sat down so we timed it rightly, could have shared a car! *Ha-ha*.'

'Yeah, well, next time,' she says, smiling.

She's eager already and hasn't even eaten yet.

The waitress gives us the menu, it doesn't take me too long to decide. I see a burger and that's enough for me to order it. I don't care what else comes with it. Tara orders the lasagne. I order a beer and she orders a glass of wine. Feels like we are a couple already.

'This place looks lovely.' She looks around as she takes off her coat. 'Looks like Tom wasn't messing with you. Even the menu, I didn't know what to choose. I wanted about five different course meals.'

'Was there? I didn't really read much of the menu, I just saw the burger and ordered that. But yeah, it is a nice place. I know I will have to be eating my words when I get back to the apartment. He'll have a smug face waiting for me when I get back.'

'So how's your week?'

'Yeah, fine. Quiet which I am grateful for because my brother is coming Friday. So, we are going to some restaurant I don't even know where it is, but he's collecting me or his friend, I don't really know. The only thing I took from the conversation is I have to be ready by seven. So, that's enough for me. How is your week?' I ask as I take a sip of my beer.

'*Ah*, yeah good, nothing really to report. One of my employees came down with a bug on Monday, so I wasn't sure if I would have to cancel this... *ahh*... dinner because I had no one to cover, but then one of the girl's concerts, I think... well... anyway, it got cancelled so she worked this evening.'

'Wow, that was lucky it got cancelled, well, lucky for me maybe not you.' I laugh.

'I know, I said to her "Are you sure it's cancelled because I don't mind cancelling my plans", but she said it was, so darn, no excuse, had to make an appearance.'

Our meal arrives. Both meals look delicious.

Tara looks at her meal and says, 'Glad I didn't cancel now; I would have missed a lovely meal.' She smirks while cutting her lasagne and glancing at me.

'Yeah, would have been a crying shame,' I say as I take a bite of my burger.

The meal was lovely, we cleared our plates and decided we would both have another drink. The evening flew I didn't even realise the time until the waitress brought down the bill. I looked at my watch and saw it was half nine and the restaurant was closing at ten.

'Jeez, the time flew; I didn't realise that was the time.'

'Yeah, me neither and we both have to be up early tomorrow. I'll have one last sip and that's enough for me.'

'I'll just take a look at the bill.'

She takes a sip of her drink while shaking her head and says, 'No, honestly, Ciaran just for tonight, I think it would be fair if we split the bill, we won't owe each other anything then.'

'Ah no, Tara, I couldn't do that. I'd never hear the end of it from Tom.'

'But you don't have to tell him. I think it would be fair on each of us if we don't want to meet again, we won't feel like we got stiffed by the other.'

'Oh, do you not want to do this again?'

'No, I mean, I'm not saying that, I'm just saying the pressure is off if we do or do not want to have another dinner. Honestly, Ciaran, if you pay, I'll just put the money in your pocket soo…' She sits back in her seat.

'OK, Tara, if I pay, I will offend you and I don't want to do that, but I don't come off well in this story.'

'But no one has to know, I'll say you paid.'

'Or you could say I paid and let me pay. That's fair and true.'

'To be honest, Ciaran, I have had three dates in the past with men who paid on the first date and there was no attraction there, so it looked like I used them for a free dinner, so I don't want to jinx this good evening.'

'OK, well, that's fair enough. So, this once, it will be split. Just once, so we don't jinx tonight.' I fooster in my pocket for money and say, 'Quick, while no one is watching, we'll both put the money in.'

Tara puts her money in first and then I put mine in. The timing was perfect because the waitress came back to take the bill. We both stand up, put on our coats and walk towards the door.

'I've just called an Uber. Do you want to share a taxi?'

'Thanks, but Tom said he'd collect me.'

'*Ah*, OK. Well, the evening was lovely. It was a nice change from cleaning tables.'

'*Ah* well, I'm glad. So, do you want to do it again?' I think it's the cold that's making me jumpy, not nerves.

'Yeah, I would,' she says, smiling. The taxi arrives and she turns back her head to acknowledge it.

'Well, I better head. Is Tom here yet?'

'Yeah, he'll be here in a few minutes, he's always punctual.'

'Oh, OK.'

She's still waiting. Is she waiting for me to attempt to kiss her so she can bat me away, or does she want me to kiss her? At least if I make a move, I'll get my answer.

I take a step slowly towards her, but she hasn't moved yet. Probably waiting for me to get close so she can give me a hard slap. My lips graze hers and I'm half waiting for the slap, but no slap comes on my cheek. So, I lean in more for a tender kiss. Her scent is so sweet. I move my head back and smile to say, 'Night, Tara.'

She smiles back and says, 'Night, Ciaran.' She turns and opens the taxi door; she takes one look back at me and smiles again before she enters the taxi.

I smile back and wave as the taxi drives off. Punctual as ever, Tom drives up and I get into the car.

'You timed that perfect.'

'Yeah, I was here a few minutes early, but I saw the two of ye at the door, so I thought I'd hang back and see what happens between the two of ye. You got a kiss, *OOOHHH*.'

'Oh whatever, leave me alone.'

'So, second date on the cards so.'

'Yeah, we'll see. Maybe, maybe not.'

'Oh, don't play it so cool, you're not fooling me.'

I think I am if you think I like her, I think to myself and smirk. Tom notices the smirk.

'*Oohhh,* aren't ya cute.'

I stare at him. 'Sorry, I know you're not gushy. Do you want me to drop you off somewhere and you can pick up a working girl to alleviate this mushiness?'

'*Haaaahaa,* maybe next time. But I have work in the morning, so I need some sleep.'

My charm worked better than I planned. I thought it would take longer for Tara to enjoy my company and fall for my appealing nature. I underestimated her vulnerability and her naivety. Are my charms that good or was the stone heart bitchiness just a defence mechanism? Maybe she liked me that night at the party and then I was rude to her, so she was disappointed that I didn't fancy her and is now grateful that I'm showing interest in her. It would make sense; it wasn't that I was rude, it was that I didn't fancy her

Chapter Eight

I'm all ready for the big night of eating and drinking with my brother and his friends. The taxi collects me at seven and my brother jumps out of it to greet me with a bear hug.

'Hey, man, it's great to see you,' he says.

'Yeah, you too. So, where are we headed?' I ask.

'Patience, brother. We just have to collect Eoin and then we will go to the bar. John is in the back. You remember John?'

I look in the back. 'Hey, John,' I say as I sit into the taxi.

'Hey, Ciaran, long time no see. How have you been?'

'Oh, fine yeah. You?'

'Yeah all right, you probably heard me and Louise broke up.'

'What, no? Gary never mentioned it. When? Why? Ye were together what *ahh...*'

'Ten years.'

I look at John and my mouth drops. 'Wow.'

'Yeah so, it's about three months now, she was seeing someone at work and then I think it got to be more than a fling so yeah, she ended things. I didn't even see it coming.'

'So how are you?'

'Yeah, getting there. The first few weeks were horrible, I didn't get out of bed most days. I was at a bar drinking and they both walked in. I was not expecting to ever see them together because it was my usual pub but not hers so—'

I interrupt, 'So you punched him?'

'No, I didn't. They didn't see me, but I just saw them laughing and holding hands and I just thought, well, she's happy so I'm not going to let myself be miserable over her. So, I got up and walked out and went to work, hung out with friends and yeah life is different. But feeling sorry for myself would never be me and I'd hate to be like that, so just have to move on and be grateful we never married or had children.'

I exhale and say, 'Fair play to you.'

Gary says from the front seat, 'So, we'll be all having a single guys' night tonight. Eoin's wife left him for her sister's brother-in-law about a year ago now.'

'What the heck? What happened to good old-fashioned the husband left the wife for his secretary, now it's the other way around.'

Gary turns his head back to us. 'Yeah, I know, 21st century women.' He puffs out air.

We pull to a stop and Eoin gets in.

'Hey, boys.'

'Hey, Eoin,' we all say.

He rubs his hands. 'So, where are we headed?'

'Not too long to wait, lads,' Gary says and gives us his iconic smug smile.

We pull outside a bar called The Kings Crown. The lighting is low so it's fair to assume that this place transforms into a late bar or nightclub in the later hours. Gary heads over to a waiter standing at the door, he says something to him and then turns back to us to signal for us to follow him.

The four of us are shown to a booth with the other three lads. We exchange pleasantries and the menus are placed on the table. Gary goes to the bar and orders four pints. Our table consists of steak, burgers and chips along with two pints each. I head up to the bar for the next round.

After I order, I turn and see Tara sitting at a table with... I tilt my head a bit further, she's with another man. She hasn't seen me so I could just walk back to our table and pretend I didn't see her. But I probably will end up looking at them during the night and then she'll spot me and wonder why I didn't come over or leave quickly to avoid an awkward encounter. I drop the pints down to the table and signal that I'm going over to a corner of the restaurant. They think nothing of it and chat among themselves.

I head over. 'Hey, Tara.'

She looks up at me and smiles; why is she smiling? 'Hey, Ciaran.' She gets up and hugs me. OK, this I was not expecting she turns to her friend. 'Ciaran, this is Paul. He works in the restaurant beside my coffee shop.' Paul holds out his hand 'Hey, man, nice to meet you.'

'Yeah, you too.' I look at Tara and I feel like I need to explain why I am here. 'I'm here with my brother Gary and his friends.' I point towards our booth.

'Oh, right, he's here for the stag, is that right?' She remembers.

'Yeah, that's right.' I look at them both again and smile 'So, did you have the food yet?'

Tara sits back and pulls up her menu. 'No, not yet, we are just about to order. Did ye eat yet?'

'Yeah, I had the steak burger and chips. It was very nice.'

She looks at the menu. 'Oh yeah, that does sound nice. Paul, what are you thinking?'

'*Hmm* yeah, and the fish looks delicious also. I'll be humming and hawing for another while I think.'

We both laugh. Tara looks at me again. I shrug my shoulder and say, 'Well, I better get back or my pint might be gone. Some of the lads drink like a fish.'

'OK, Ciaran. *Ahh*, I'll see you again.'

Is she brushing me off or was there an emphasis on the "again"?

'Yeah, I'll chat you again.' I turn to Paul. 'It was nice meeting you.'

'Yeah, you too.'

'Enjoy your meal.' I smile. They both say 'Thanks' and I head back to the lads.

Gary looks at me, confused. 'Hey, where did you go?'

I sit down. 'Oh, I just went to say hi to a friend.'

'*Ohh*, which friend, where is she or he?'

I look at Gary. 'SHE is over by the window with a friend she knows.'

Gary puts his head outside the booth to have a look. '*OOHH* she's pretty, how do you know her?'

'Oh, she's friends with Tom's girlfriend.'

'Oh.' He looks at me. 'You look a bit bothered. What's up?'

'Nothing.' I take a gulp of my pint.

'Ohh, I know that move. You are bothered she's out with him. Why? Are ye kind of seeing one another?'

'No.'

'Right, but you want to see her?'

'No, we just went out and had fun. That's all. She didn't mention him or that she had plans tonight.'

'Well, maybe she didn't, and it was a spur-of-the-moment thing.'

'Yeah maybe, anyway.' I hold up my pint and say, 'Here's to a good night.' We clink our glasses and say 'cheers'.

I don't care if she's out or that she's out with a man, but I'm just confused and disappointed. I thought she was succumbing to my charms, maybe I was wrong.

Chapter Nine

I wake the next morning. I get my phone to check the time. It's nine o'clock and my head feels terrible. I go back to sleep again. I wake at twelve and I see I got a message from Tara. Well, not a message, it's a funny photo with a dog in sunglasses lying down with a caption that says, 'not able to play today'.

I send back smiley faces. I think back to the previous night. After my fourth drink, I looked to see if Tara was still there, but she was gone. I look at my phone and hope I didn't send her a drunk message. *Phew,* I didn't. Now I know, I left my phone at the apartment because I didn't need it. I wasn't going to be leaving Gary all night. So that was lucky.

I don't know why, but I decide to ring Tara. She's probably working which suits me because I would prefer if she saw the missed call than have to talk to her.

Ring ring ring ring. 'Hello?' *Crap!* She picked up.

I'm rubbing my head and say in a hoarse voice, 'Hey, Tara, it's Ciaran.'

'I know. Hey, Ciaran. How was your night?'

'Yeah, it was good, think I drank too much because I feel terrible, and my throat is so dry.'

'Yeah, you sound hoarse.'

'Yeah, think I just need to drink water and maybe eat something. Listen, me and the lads were talking last night, and they mentioned there was a good film in the cinema so I am wondering if you would like to go?'

'Yeah, sure, when?' *Well, that was easy.*
'*Ah*, tonight. Would that suit?'
'Yeah. I'll be off at half five.'
'OK cool. I'll check the times and message you.'
'Grand.'
'OK, Tara, bye.'
'Bye, Ciaran.'

OK, so it seems she is still interested. Maybe she's keeping her options open. *Argh,* why did I go out last night?

I check the timetable; the movie starts at half eight. That's a perfect time; it's not too early and not too late. I hope it's good or at least watchable. I text Tara the time and she says she'll meet me there. I arrive at 8.15, but Tara beats me there. She's sitting in the lobby and smiles when she sees me.

'Hey, Ciaran!'
'Hey, Tara, sorry were you waiting long?'
'No about five minutes. I have the tickets and I was just about to get the popcorn.'
'What? You got the tickets? But I invited you.'
'Oh well, I didn't buy them, one of my friends gave them to me ages ago. She won them in a raffle, so I decided why not use them tonight because they only last six months.'
'Oh, right, well, I'll get the popcorn and what drink do you want?'
'Diet Coke is fine, thanks.'

We take our seats a few rows up the steps, and I am grateful that it's not full of people. She hasn't asked me about my dinner with Gary and I haven't asked her about Paul. I'm watching the film, but all I can think about is why hasn't she mentioned her date or not date.

Tara whispers to me, 'That actor looks familiar. Do you

know what film he was in?'

I'm not even sure which actor she is talking about. But I say, 'Yeah, he does look familiar, *ugh*, can't think now.'

'It will probably come to me in a minute or when the film is over, *ha-ha*.' Tara laughs and takes a handful of popcorn.

We are walking out of the cinema when Tara looks at me and says, 'What did you think of the film?'

I turn and say, '*Hm?* Oh the film, yeah, I liked it. The ending was good.' I'm fumbling in my jacket pocket.

'Are you all right?'

'Yeah, I'm fine, sorry. I was making sure I had my wallet. What did you think of the film?'

'It was good, I'd definitely recommend it to my friends.'

'Hmm, would you recommend it to Paul?'

'Paul? Probably not; he likes romcoms and scary films.'

I look at her confused, hoping she'll explain how she knows this.

'I know they're total opposites; it's such a contradiction.'

'So, you know Paul well?'

'Ah yeah, well, like since I opened anyway. I met his girlfriend first because she was one of my first customers. Then Paul and I worked the same shifts so we do a thing where if we are off at the same time, we go to a restaurant for a meal and drink.'

'Oh, that's nice. And his girlfriend doesn't mind you two going for meals and drinks?'

'No, course not. They've been dating for years, and I would never go near a man who has a partner, way too much drama.'

'*Hmmm.*'

She looks at me. 'Why? Would it bother you? Did it bother

you?'

'No, it didn't bother me. I just wasn't expecting to see you in the restaurant and definitely wasn't expecting to see you having dinner with a man.'

'A man! I was having dinner with a friend which is allowed.'

'It is allowed. I'm not saying that. *Argh!* I'm just saying I wasn't expecting it and then I wasn't sure if you were seeing other people or maybe you were seeing him and planning on seeing me on the side for options.'

Tara looks at me going from shocked to disgusted. OK, I crossed a line. I know I did.

'WHAT? How could you assume all that in just one dinner? What the heck? Easy to see how stories spread when one innocent meal can lead to people assuming and spreading gossip. Instant assumptions. Jeez, Ciaran, like you have met me a handful of times and asked me out yet you just assume then that I'm capable of seeing other people on the side. For one, where would I get the time to see all these men and, secondly, what the heck gives you the right to judge what I do in my personal time? Is it that now you have entered my life, I should just work and see you and that should be enough for me, and I should be grateful you entered my life and made it better?'

'No, it's not that. Look, I'm sorry, Tara, I did jump to conclusions, and I shouldn't have.'

'No, you shouldn't have. I don't know what type of women you saw in the past or are still seeing, but I am not one for playing the field.'

'I'm sorry, Tara, I'm judging you by my own standards and that's not fair. And... *Ah...* just for the record, I'm not seeing anyone. Well, apart from you, I hope.'

There's an awkward pause as we stare at each other. She

breaks the silence.

'Look, it's fine. Let's just move on. Look, I have to go back to the café to check the orders. So, if you want to call it a night, that's fine.'

'*Ah*, no, it's fine. I'll go back with you. Besides, it's late for you to be in a café on your own.'

'Oh, quite a gentleman. It's not like I never stayed late at the café before.'

'Yeah, but that was before me.' I give her my iconic smile.

'Right. OK, whatever.'

We walk over to my car and drive in silence.

Tara opens the door to her café and heads straight into her little cubicle behind the counter.

'Sorry, just have to do this while it's all fresh in my head,' she shouts from behind the cubicle and continues, 'I'll make the coffee when I'm finished.'

'It's fine, Tara, I can make it.'

I go to switch on the coffee machine and while it's heating up, I lean against the counter and look around. I never noticed all the little ornaments and flowers in her café. There are pink, orange and yellow roses over by the window.

'You have nice flowers over by the window. I never noticed them before. They look fresh. Have you an admirer?' I joke but realise quickly that I shouldn't have said that considering what happened between us like fifteen minutes ago.

'Oh yeah, thanks. They are my favourite flowers. No, they are fake. It's just handier to have fake ones because the real ones don't last that long, and I'd be forever buying new ones.' She either chose to ignore my admirer comment or didn't hear me. Well, I'm glad either way.

When the coffee is made, I bring the cups over to a table.

Tara comes out as soon as the cups are placed on the table.

'Now, sorry about that. You had to make your own coffee. I'm not a great host, am I?' She takes her cup and takes a sip. I hope it's all right. Making coffee for someone who owns a café. It's like cooking for a chef.

'It's fine, Tara. I may as well be at something while I wait for you. How's the coffee?'

'It's nice, yeah, thanks. Would you be interested in a job here? You can put your CV in the letter box.'

'I'll think about it, no harm to have a back-up plan in case the teaching doesn't work out.'

'Yeah exactly. For me, my backup plan is bookkeeping.' She laughs.

'What? You did bookkeeping?'

'Yeah, I did, that was my degree, but then this opportunity came. I used to work here, and the manager was retiring so he told me to go for his job and that the people who owned this place were selling and I should consider it because I had great ideas. When I worked here, I would run ideas with the manager and he said, "If I owned it, I would take all your ideas, but the owners just have the mantra if it's not broke, don't fix it." So yeah, that's how I ended up here.'

'Wow, it's mad how life can change and in your case change for the better. With me, I just wanted fixed hours and holidays, that's the only reason I finished my degree.'

Tara's phone rings. 'Oh sorry.' She looks at her phone. 'Oh, it's Haley. Hi, Haley, how are you?'

'Yeah, that's me, I'm here. OK thanks, you're very good. Bye, thanks again.'

'Problem?'

'No, that was a woman who owns the clothes shop across the road, she saw the light was on in here and was worried someone was breaking in or... shacking up.'

'Great that everyone looks out for each other around here,' I say, trying to contain a yawn.

'I know, it is nice. Here, I'll take that and wash up and you can head off and get sleep. Thanks for bringing me here.'

I stand to put on my jacket. 'No problem, how are you getting home?'

She walks to the sink and runs water. 'Oh, I'll call a taxi, one of the lads I know will be working tonight.'

'I can take you home. You won't be long washing up, so I don't mind waiting another minute or two.'

'No, its fine, Ciaran. Thanks, though.'

'Come on, I'm here, use me. My car is outside, and you won't be waiting. The weirdos come out after 11 so...'

'OK fine, thanks. I'll just leave these draining and I'll get my coat and keys and follow you out.'

I drop her off outside her house. I'm hoping she won't invite me in because I will have to refuse because I'm so tired, but she might see it as rejection.

'Thanks, Ciaran. I'd invite you in, but I think you are tired, and I am tired so I would be bad company. It sounds lame, I know, but it's true.'

'That's fine, Tara. To be honest, I am tired so I probably would have passed out on your couch. I know I'm getting old when I'm looking forward to a bed just to sleep in. I've become so lame.'

I look at her and I think I may have offended her. 'I mean, I'm lame now, not you.'

'No, I am lame, but at this point in my life, I don't mind it. I had my fun and now I'm happy to get early nights and enjoy the early mornings.'

She kisses me on the cheek and says, 'Night, Ciaran.'

'Night, Tara.'

Chapter Ten

It's been a busy week for both me and Tara. Two of her employees were out sick on two different days so she had to cover for them and try and do her books. I was busy with schoolwork and organising the sports day that was held on Friday. We finally were able to go on a date tonight. I offered to collect her, but Tara suggested we go to a restaurant near her place. I'm not sure if it was a good suggestion or a bad one.

This date is going well; it's only twenty minutes in but already better than the second. I picked her up at her house and presented her with flowers; roses, orange and yellow. Which showed I listen. I followed her to her door so she could put them in water straight away. I looked around her house and it is very girly in that there are pink and purple colours in the kitchen and sitting room. Maybe her room will be black to alleviate the girly girl exterior of this house. She smiles when putting the flowers on the table and says, 'So, shall we head off?'

'Yep, ready when you are.' I lead her out her door, but she turns to lock it. Not quite the masculine exit, but it is her house so the locking up would be normal for any homeowner.

The restaurant she chose is a five-minute walk from her house. There's a maitre d who asks if we have a table booked or if we would like a table. Tara takes the lead and gives her name. From there, we are escorted to our table. Either she is always prepared or was here before so knew a booked table would be faster to eat because the place is very busy.

I decided to find out. 'So, were you ever here before?'

She's pouring the water into both our glasses. '*Hmm*, yeah, a few times, with friends, once with an ex but it didn't last long and then I came here with my brother and Rachel.'

'Oh, right, so it was the restaurant that sealed the decision with the ex, was it?'

'*Haaa* yeah, he didn't like the food so in my mind we were finished. He turned left and I turned right for home.'

'Pressure is on so, good thing you warned me. I'll be *hmm* and awing my food.'

A waiter gives us our menu, he smiles at Tara and me.

'So, any suggestions? Or would you recommend something that isn't as delicious to see my reaction?'

'*Ha* I was thinking about doing that, but no, I will let you choose your meal. I believe in equal rights and wrongs.' She smiles at this remark.

'*Haaa*, OK, so you are saying I'm free to make up my own mind and thus responsible for my own mistakes.'

'Yeah, more or less.'

I laugh and say, 'Very grateful!' The waiter comes over and we order.

We are onto our dessert now. I had the beef, and it was very tasty and tender, I'm proud I made a good decision. Tara had steak and from her face, I could assume that was also delicious. Judging from the way she cut into it and the wine she chose, I'm sure she had it before. We both had the same dessert which was apple tart and cream. We probably could have done the couple thing and shared spoons and ordered one, but I like my own dessert and I think Tara does too.

When our dessert is taken away, I tell Tara I'm going to the bathroom, but I go to the bar instead and pay for our meal while also ordering a drink each for us. I bring the two down to the table and Tara looks surprised but not disgusted so she is happy for this night to continue.

'Now here we are.' I set the two drinks down on the table.

'Thanks, Ciaran, I called for the bill, but he hasn't come back with it. We can half it, it's fair.'

I just look at her, she knows I am about to say something.

'What?'

'*Ah,* not to offend your feminism but I paid for the meal when I went to buy these.' I gesture to the two drinks.

'Oh really, me thinking you were going to the bathroom. I'll try that trick next time. Thanks, but the steak was dearer than your meal, I wouldn't have ordered it if I thought you'd pay for the lot, sorry.'

I hold my two hands up to indicate for her to stop. 'It's fine, you enjoyed it. If you left half of it behind, I'd be tempted to only pay half it, so it worked out well that you ate it all. No awkwardness of telling you to pay for the uneaten half.'

'Thanks for doing that and for the drinks.' She grabs her drink and takes a sip.

We finish our drinks, put on our coats and head for the door. I'm not sure what time it is but I think it's too late to go to another pub. I subtly allow Tara to lead the rest of the night.

We are both walking out the door and down the steps and I am wondering if I should turn left and allow her to turn right.

'So, do you want to come back for coffee, or do you want to go somewhere? Some of the girls are drinking in a pub it's about a fifteen-minute walk.'

She's letting me choose; if I choose her place, she will think I only want one thing and if I say the friends, she'll think I'm planning on looking elsewhere. I really can't choose without losing somehow.

'I think I'll head home, Tara. I'm a bit tired.' Neutral ground, choose neither. What will she do with this decision?

'Oh, OK, thanks for dinner, Ciaran. I had a great night.' She looks disappointed.

'Yeah, me too.' I turn to walk away and so does she. I can't leave it like this. I turn and follow Tara.

'Tara!'

She turns. 'Yeah?'

'If I chose your place, you would think I'm after something and if I chose your friends, you would think I'm after someone. So, I didn't know what to choose. But if I had to choose without fear of offending you, then I would choose your place so I just thought I would tell you and yeah, so, goodnight.'

I turn to head the way I was going, even though I don't know where I am going.

'Hey, wait.' Tara pulls my arm and smiles. 'Back to mine it is.'

It is starting to get chilly out, so I am glad Tara lives so close to the restaurant. She opens the door and heads straight into the kitchen to pour water into the kettle.

I sit at the table and take off my coat. When she has the kettle full and boiling, she turns to me and takes off her coat. 'Sorry, I just need a hot drink to warm me up, it's so cold now.'

'Yeah, happy to have a hot drink. My hands are so cold.'

'Yeah, mine too.' Without thinking, we are feeling each other's hands. Hers are just as cold as mine. This feels so natural, we just take our hands away and Tara asks, 'Tea or coffee?'

'Ah, tea. Thanks.' She pours the water into the cups. I notice she is having tea too.

'Now here we are, free of charge.' She smiles while saying

it.

'*Awh*, how nice, the charge will come next time.'

'Yeah.'

The tea is really warming me up and the conversation is flowing about our meal and the snaps she keeps getting from her friends. Have they never gone out before that they have to share every sordid detail of the night? *Grrr*, I can't stand that small-minded crap.

'Sorry, I don't know why they send me these photos; I barely go on this app.'

'Maybe they are trying to tell you that you should have blown me off and gone out with them instead.'

'*Haaa*, yeah maybe that is it. Oh well, next time I will do that. But for now, I suppose your company will have to do.'

'Yeah, suppose it will, poor you.'

She takes our cups and puts them in the sink. I don't want the night to be over yet, but there's nothing left to drink.

'I have a nice bottle of wine in the sitting room if you want to try it. They say red wine is nicer and warm, so I left it in there.'

Hmm, she wants me to stay.

'Yeah, cool.'

'Great, I'll get the glasses, you head in.' I hear the clinking of glasses as I take a seat on the couch.

'Now, *ah*, where did I leave the bottle? *Ah*, there it is.' She goes over to a chair near the radiator.

She opens the bottle and pours a generous amount of wine into both our glasses. She wants me to stay awhile, it seems.

She joins me on the couch. I think it was instinctive as opposed to purpose because she gets comfy quickly. She holds her glass up towards mine and says, 'Cheers.'

'Yeah, cheers.' We take a sip of the wine. 'Oh, that is nice.'

I look at the glass and then at her. She seems pleased and must have chosen the wine herself. I take another sip of wine.

I don't know how this happened, but we ended up kissing on the couch. We drank nearly the full bottle and given we had a few drinks in the restaurant, I think we are both slightly intoxicated to care how this happened.

She tastes of wine and steak. I move to her neck, and it smells of flowers and wine. It's enthralling and I want to taste more of it. I move my hand up to her neck for closer grip. She seems to like it because she is even pushing it into my lips while her hands are tightening into my back. My other hand is slowly moving under her top towards her breast, but she stops me and pulls away. Maybe I have gone too far.

She looks at me and I am unsure of what happens next. She takes both my hands and brings me into her bedroom. OK, so this is happening, she wants it and I want it. Good thing I came prepared. She sits on the bed while holding my hand, I am about to join her when she pulls at my pants. OK, I know where this is headed, and I have no complaints that she wants to start with me. She looks at me as she slowly undoes my belt and opens my pants button, she unbuttons the last three buttons of my shirt. She can see now I am ready and looks pleased. She slowly lowers my boxers and I step out of them. She looks at me again and then slowly moves her head towards me, I feel her mouth there and I gasp. She uses her hand to hold me and moves her mouth further into me. She is moving fast, and I feel myself pulsate inside her mouth, she moves her mouth slightly back and flicks her tongue around my tip.

'*AHHH,* Tara, I am going to…' And this sends me over the top. I grip her head tighter as she moves faster into me again and finally I unload inside her mouth. '*OOOOOOHHHH!* Fuck, Tara.'

She looks up when I am out of her mouth, and I feel like collapsing. I kneel on the floor and bring her face towards me and start kissing her mouth. Our tongues meet, and it is magic. Every bit of her I want in my mouth. I kiss her neck and lift her top over her head and kiss her shoulder, her arm and then I move to the other side. And finally, I reach her back and undo her bra and kiss and suck her left nipple and then her right. She gasps and tilts back her head. I pull her up and sit her on the bed, I undo the button in her jeans and slowly move them off her legs. She stands quickly and sits back down again. I pull off her pants and toss them on the floor. I move my hand up slowly towards her inner thigh. I stop then to look at her. She stares and says nothing, I keep moving my hand towards her knickers, I pull them to one side and put one finger between her lips. She gasps louder, she feels so wet. My hand moves to her hips and grab her knickers. She stands quickly again and allows me to take them off. She steps out of them and sits again. I pull her thighs apart and she groans, her breathing is deep and fast. I move my mouth closer to her clit and put my tongue in while I move my hand to her sex and put two fingers inside her and start to move fast while licking her clit faster and keeping her thighs apart. She's panting, moving with the rhythm of my pace. Her hands are holding onto the duvet cover. I can feel her body start to shake. She lets out a loud groan and her whole body falls onto the bed. I remove my head from her and watch her lying on the bed. Her breathing starts to slow, and she looks up at me. She sits up slightly and smiles. She grabs the back of my neck and pulls my face towards hers. Our lips meet and we kiss deeper and longer. She pulls back and asks, 'Are you ready?' I nod and she follows with 'Do you have condoms?' I nod again and move off her to grab a condom from my pants pocket. I look at her as I roll it on. Her eyes brighten and our lips touch again, harder this time. I slide into her slowly and she groans. I kiss her tenderly and pull out, then I move into her faster and she gasps. My hands move to find hers and I move fast inside her as she matches my pace. I want her and I want this so bad. Our speed quickens and I can feel I am about to come. I hope Tara feels this too because I can't control myself any longer. Oh, I can feel this release is coming and '*AAAHHHHHHH! OOHHH GOOOODDD, TARA!*'

She shouts my name too and we both collapse at the same time.

OH MY GOD, THAT WAS UNBELIEVABLE. I wonder did she feel it too. Well, by the sound she made, I am guessing she enjoyed it. We don't speak for a few minutes, our bodies catching up with our breathing. Finally, I look down at her and she is smiling, looking up at me. We kiss each other tenderly and I lie down beside her, holding her hand.

Chapter Eleven

The next morning, I wake up and notice the duvet cover is different and it hits me... I slept with Tara last night. She's not in the bed beside me. *Hmmm*... I wonder has she left me a note. I sit up and look at the pillow. No, no note there. I look at the locker and nothing. Then I hear noise in the kitchen. *Ah*, she didn't leave at all; must be cooking me breakfast as a thank you for last night. Well, no problem; Tara turned out to be a good night for me too. If she gets all clingy, I'll be breaking up with her sooner than I thought though. I get my phone out and check what date I have in mind. *Ah* good, another few weeks or so before I end things.

I better go out to the kitchen in case she plans on breakfast in bed. If I go out in my boxers, she might think I'm looking for round two and that's not what a gentleman would do and, anyway, I'm cold, so I'll put on my clothes.

Crap! Can't find my shoes, oh yes, they're in the sitting room. I took them off there last night before we got busy.

I go out to the kitchen and Tara is on the phone. She turns as soon as I sit and smiles at me.

'Yeah, OK, Mum. I'll talk to you later, bye.

'Hey! Sorry, that was my mother, I'm meeting her later. One of her colleagues is getting married and she wants to go outfit shopping for it.' She goes to the press to take out a cup.

'Actually, Tara, orange juice would be great if you have it, I just feel like something refreshing.'

'Oh yeah, no problem.' She puts the cup back and gets a glass and pours the orange juice. I think I will drink all of that in a second.

'Thanks.' I drink it all down. '*Ahhh!*'

She smiles. I'm on the defensive immediately. 'What? Sorry, that was rude.'

'No, it's fine. Do you want another glass?'

I look at the glass. 'Ah, yeah, I would. Thanks.'

She pours more into the glass.

'So, what's so funny, do I drink weird?'

'No, I'm only laughing 'cos normally, I leave water in my room but last night I didn't, and it was probably the most time it was needed.'

'Yeah, definitely worked up a thirst last night and an appetite.' I'm just after realising what I said and waiting for the awkward pause, but Tara laughs, and I laugh too. *Phew!* That could have gone another way.

'Oh, sorry. I cooked rashers and eggs, so I'm glad you have an appetite,' she says cheekily.

She turns, opens the oven door and takes out a tray of rashers, sausages and fried eggs. She puts bread into the toaster and takes two plates from the press along with a knife and fork each from a nearby drawer. I would help, but I don't want to feel like we are becoming a couple in sync with one another. That kind of thing gives me the shivers.

The breakfast was perfect, it filled the huge hole in my stomach. I offer to clean up because that's not a cheesy couple task, that's just good manners. It didn't take that much effort as our plates were cleared so I just put the plates and cutlery in the dishwasher and Tara wiped the table. Job done. I go to get my jacket and Tara calls me back.

'*Ah,* hey, before you leave, do you want coffee or tea, I was gonna make one for myself.' She gestures towards the kettle.

I'm fixing the collar in my jacket looking at her. 'It's fine if you are in a hurry, it's just the way I was brought up; always offer a beverage.' She smiles and leans against the counter.

I should just leave. 'Amm… yeah. OK, that'll warm me up before I head out in that.' We both look out the window to the blue sky and the sun's heat radiating through the living area and burst laughing. Tara takes two cups from the press and asks, 'So, what are you up to today?'

I take off my jacket and take my previous seat. 'Well, not much, I'm just going to the pub with Tom later to watch a match – he loves soccer – and then I think we are meeting Megan and her friends later.' I try to hold back a yawn, but I can't.

'Yeah, I'm tired too,' Tara says as she brings over the cups, 'and I have to go into the café in half an hour to go over the books. I just feel like sleeping.' She takes a sip of her tea.

'Yeah, I think with the wine and the other stuff' – I try to stop smiling – 'it's having an effect on us this morning.' I take a sip of my coffee, a long sip to wait and see what she will say.

'Yeah, I had a good time last night and I'm not just talking about the bedroom stuff, the whole night was great.'

I can see it in her eyes she's genuine, I almost feel bad. 'Yeah, I had a great time too.' I take one more sip of my coffee and stand up to put on my coat. 'I'd like to see you tonight again only Tom had this arranged.'

'No, it's fine, I'm busy anyway.' She stands to take both cups.

OK, doesn't seem like she wants to elaborate, and I can't ask because it will make me sound domineering and jealous, so I'll just let it pass, she might tell me another time. I'm not quite sure if I should go over to kiss her goodbye or stay standing and say something nice. So, I pretend I'm trying to zip up my jacket.

'Sorry, I'll get the door; the lock opens a weird way.' She goes to the door, unlocks it and opens it.

What do I do here? I stand in front of her and take her hand. 'I really had fun last night, Tara; can I call you to make other plans?'

She smiles; this was a good idea. 'Yeah, I had fun too, Ciaran. Maybe we can do something some night during the week?'

'Yeah sure, great.' I kiss her on the cheek and smile at her. 'Bye, Tara.'

Whoo, that was fun, time for a break and to join the real world.

Chapter Twelve

'Ciaran! Ciaran! Wake up!'

I hear Tom's voice; I open my eyes and he's standing right in my face. 'What is it?' I demand.

'Remember we are going to watch the match.'

I sit up quickly. 'Right, yeah, what time is that?'

'In an hour.'

'Oh, plenty of time to go back to sleep.' I slant back down and pull the covers over my head.

'No, come on, get up. We'll eat something before we go.'

'All right, I'll be up in a minute.'

'Why are you so tired? Oh, right, up all night with Tara, how's it going with her?'

'Yeah, fine,' I say with my eyes closed.

'So did ye have fun last night?'

I open my eyes and smile. 'Yeah, we did.'

'*Oooh*, Ciaran, my man, so suppose that's the end of it so you got your bit of action and on to the next one.'

OK, I'm wide awake now, not going to be able to go back to sleep. I sit up and rub my eyes. 'Actually, no… I'm meeting her again one of the nights during the week.'

'What? And on a weeknight too. *Ohhh*, you must be sort of liking her anyway.' He taps me on the back.

'No, I don't know, she's fine and I'm not at anything else soo… may as well see her for another while.'

'Not at anything? We're going drinking tonight, another

chance to meet someone else. I don't know, I think you are making excuses.' He eyes me questionably.

'I don't know, I'll see for another while anyway.'

But he is right, I would have been on to another only for the plan. I hope Megan's friends are ugly and mostly men out tonight because I won't be able to stick Tom talking to me like I'm falling for Tara and that bullshit of being a changed man because of her. But if there is a nice woman out tonight, I could get the number anyway, Tara would never know.

The match is over, and Tom is delighted; his team won by two goals. We have another drink and then head to meet Megan and her friends; Tom says it's one of the friends' birthday.

We enter the pub and can't seem to see Megan; Tom sends her a message.

'Ah crap!' Tom shakes his head.

'What?'

'We are in the wrong pub, I thought she said the King's Road, but it's the Rosebud Lane.'

'Ah that's like another fifteen-minute walk, we'll have one here and then go and meet them.'

'Yeah OK, I'll just text her that we'll be there soon.' While Tom is texting, I go to the bar, order drinks and give him a nod to get a seat.

I bring the pints down and Tom leaves his phone on the table.

'So, how are you and Megan getting on? I don't think we talked much about your relationship.'

Tom takes a sip of his pint and looks at me quizzically.

'I have been seeing Megan for the last six months and this is the first time you asked me that, what's up with you? Being considerate, I don't like it. Might have to get used to it if this is the effect Tara is having on you, you should keep her another while.'

'Yeah, we'll see.' I won't be keeping her long.

'Anyway, yeah things are going well, really like her, she's nice and funny and easy-going. You know what, the four of us should go out for a night just for a few drinks or dinner, something like that. Megan was asking me about ye before so she can see it herself and save asking me questions because she doesn't believe me when I say you don't talk much about it.'

'*Ah*, I don't know, Tom, it might be weird or look like I'm pressuring her into making this official. Tara can be a bit standoffish.'

'Well, look, ask her anyway; well, mention Megan and say she's badgering me about going for drinks so make it seem she'd be helping me out.'

I take another sip of my pint. 'Yeah, OK, I'll say it to her anyway.'

'Great, that will keep Megan off my case; she likes the two of ye so she hopes it will work out.'

'Ah really, that makes both of us.'

I'm trying to hide my smirk, so I get up to go to the bathroom.

I wake up the next morning and I can't remember a thing about last night. My head is killing me, and I feel like I'm going to be sick. I sit up and turn to put my feet on the ground and I feel it, my stomach is weird and I feel dizzy, I need the bathroom. I run to the toilet, and everything comes up. I'm afraid to leave the toilet.

'Hey, Ciaran, you OK?'

My eyes are closed when I barely answer Tom. 'No, oh my

god, what did I drink last night? How are you not as bad as me?'

'Oh, I was, I was up all night getting sick, then I drank a bit of water and took a Panadol and lay down in bed. I just got what you feel now about six hours earlier.'

'Oh my god, do you remember anything about last night? What way was I with Megan's friends?'

'To be honest, I don't even know how I was with her friends. I was expecting to see angry texts from Megan, but I didn't get anything. Well, I got one saying hope you feel better in the morning so I could have gotten sick in the pub. I hope not though, that would be embarrassing.'

I laugh lightly because I feel if I move, I will be sick. 'Yeah, that would be embarrassing.'

'Thanks for the support, I was going to bring you water but nah won't bother now.'

I raise my hand in the air. 'No wait, please, I'm sorry. I'm sure I made more of a fool of myself than you. Please, I need a bit of water, my stomach feels like crap.'

'Oh fine, the novelty has worn off seeing you look so miserable, I'll be right back.'

'Thanks.'

Tom comes back in the room within twenty seconds. 'Oh, thanks.' I move slowly and sit against the sink and take a sip of the water.

'You feeling any better?'

'Yeah, a small bit, but I think it helps that my stomach has gotten rid of every bit of drink that was in my body.' I take another sip of water.

Toms's phone dings. 'Oh, an Instagram photo put up by Megan.' He looks at it and then laughs and puts his hand up to his mouth. 'Oh my god, we look so drunk.'

'What? Show!'

He shows me the photo, there's like four of Megan's friends then Megan, Tom and myself. I have my arms around two girls and surprise surprise, the nice guy Tom is, even when drunk has one arm around Megan.

'Oh god! We look so drunk. My eyes look terrible!'

'*Ha ha*, how did we get so bad? Oh, there's more photos, slide over and... *Hahaha*, oh my god, look!'

There's a photo of me kissing Megan's friend on the cheek. Tom scrolls again and, oh crap, there's me in the middle and two of her friends kissing my cheeks and I have a big smile on my face, but I look so drunk.

I look at Tom. 'Oh my god! Tom, do you think I got with one of her friends?' Those photos have knocked the sickness out of me.

Tom is looking at his phone. 'What? No, I don't think so. If you did, Megan would have rung me to give out about you. It's a girl thing, isn't it? Your friend hurt my friend so I would have gotten that call.'

I stare into space. 'Yeah, but I could have gotten with one of them out of sight and Megan may not know yet.' I put my head in my hands. 'Oh crap! I can't remember, damn.'

'Hey, don't worry, Ciaran, it could be fine. It looks like we all hung out together last night, so it could just be what is shown in the photos.'

'*Grrr,* can't believe I messed up and I was so close.'

'Close to what?' Tom looks confused.

I take my head out of my hands. 'Oh well, close to being the good guy I want to be for Tara.'

'Wow, you must like her so.'

'Yeah, I really do.'

Tom smiles at me like he believes me and can't believe I felt this way. Nailed it!

'Look, Ciaran, I am sure it is OK, but I can call Megan now and see if you want.'

I look at Tom and think. 'No, it's OK, Tom, I'll just wait and see because it may just be those photos. And I can't deal with it right now anyway because I think I need to go back to bed. Help me up, will ya?'

Tom pulls me up and I slowly walk back to bed put the covers over my head and try to sleep and not think that I messed things up so soon to D-day.

Chapter Thirteen

There's buzzing in my dream and then I open my eyes. I hear the buzzing again. What is that? I look around, it's my phone. *CRAP!* Where did I leave it? I see it on the floor, I'm hoping it isn't Tara calling to end things. No, it's Dad.

'Hey, Dad.' I yawn as I say it.

'Hey, Ciaran, were you asleep?'

'Yeah, I feel a bit sick.'

'Oh, what's up with you?'

'Oh, nothing really. Self-inflicted; I was out with Tom last night and mixed my drink so feel like crap at the minute.'

'*Ah*, no sympathy from me.'

'I know, so what's up?'

'I was just calling to ask if you would go online and look up cheap places in Spain; I want to bring your mother away for her birthday.'

'Dad, that's like two months away and Spain is nearly always cheap.'

'Yeah, well, I like to be organised, so will you do that please and let me know the numbers and I might get you to book them too because I'm not as good as you on the Internet.'

'Yeah, fine, Dad. When do you want to book?'

'Well, the end of the week and then I'll pick and get you to book.'

'Grand.'

'OK, so any other news?'

'No, Dad, very boring.'

'Oh right, no woman on the scene?'

'No, why?'

'Oh, just someone saw you having dinner with a woman.'

'Which someone?'

'I'm not telling, I was just wondering if it was true.'

'Yeah, I probably was. A friend, I know her years.' Not lying there.

'Oh right, is she nice?'

'Yeah, she's nice and she's a friend.' My tone quietens him.

'All right, well, you'll do that anyway for me, won't you?'

'Yes, I will, I'll even have a quick look now.' I start opening Safari on my phone.

'Is there any place in Spain you want to go? You know, it's a big country.'

'The south, your mother loves the heat, so somewhere along there.'

'OK.' That narrows it down!

'All right, I'll talk to you later.'

'Yeah, bye, Dad.'

I go into my messages and no text or call from Tara; I'm taking that as a good sign.

There's a tap at my door. 'Hey, Ciaran, are you awake?'

'Yeah. Just about.'

The door opens and Tom has his phone in his hand.

I look at him. 'What? Did something happen?'

He puts his phone in his pocket. '*Ah*, no, not really, I was talking to Megan there and she didn't say anything, just that it was a good night and... she brought up dinner with the four of us and apparently you were so excited about it and took out your phone and booked a meal for Friday night at Rex's.' He smiles nervously.

'What?' I take out my phone and go to calls. I look at Tom. 'I didn't call them.'

'Yeah, you went online and booked.' I go through my Internet browser and see the website then I look at my mail and see confirmation; 11.34 last night.

'Oh, crap.'

'Yeah, so that's happening.'

I look at him 'Yeah and FECK, Rex's is dear, it's like eight euros for a pint, think their cheapest dinners are eighteen euros.' I lie my head back on the pillow. 'Oh damn, you alcohol.' I shoot up. 'I'm not drinking again, where does it get you? If I was sober, I wouldn't have taken those photos and would have gone home early before I started talking about dinner plans. OH CRAP!'

I feel like Tom has something else to say. 'What?'

'Think you should look at your WhatsApp.'

'Why?'

He says nothing, just looks down tapping his foot. I look and see *Tara dinner with Megan and Tom on Friday if you want to join, 8 o'clock at Rex's.* She replied with a thumbs up.

I look at Tom. 'Ah crap, well, I'll be drinking water that night.'

Tom ever the encouraging man: 'It will be fine, Ciaran, it's just food and the four of us there, plenty of conversation and then Megan will leave us alone. I'll mention to Megan that ye are not exclusive, it makes you uncomfortable and you don't like to feel pressurised and I'm sure Tara would feel the same. Plenty of other things we can talk about.'

'Yeah, thanks, Tom, make it very clear.' I hold his stare. I hope he does.

Chapter Fourteen

I run quick to the door. I am absolutely drenched, it is pouring rain outside, I stayed late at school to finish all the correcting of tests and I wanted to change things around in the classroom and put up new posters. It's half five, plenty of time to eat and shower for tonight.

I take off my coat when I get in and go into the kitchen.

'Hey, Ciaran.' I hear Tom shout from his room.

'Hey, Tom.'

He comes into the kitchen 'Wet enough for you?'

'Yeah, I am absolutely drenched.' I wipe my pants like that will stop the water from soaking through. 'I'm just going to make a quick sandwich and then shower. Are you ready?'

Tom looks at himself, like he had to check if he was. 'Ah, yeah, more or less, I'll just change my shirt and yeah, I'm ready. I showered this morning, and I was in before the rain came, so I'm just finishing up some emails from work and then I'll be ready. We have plenty of time anyway, thankfully we are not women, they've probably started an hour ago.' He laughs as if he's proud of the joke.

'Yeah, although to be fair, they don't go too heavy on the makeup and hair, but then that could take more effort to look effortless; it's a vicious circle. Suppose not everyone is born good looking like us,' I look at him as I put the bread in the toaster. He swats his hair back.

'I know. Some people will never understand how easy we

have it, *haha!*' he stays, standing at the door and then says, 'Anyway, I better finish these emails, so I think we have time enough going at quarter to, right?'

I take ham out of the fridge. 'Oh yeah, Tara said she has to stay at the café till seven, so I wouldn't be surprised if she's like a half hour late. Although she said ten minutes late, but I'd say more.'

'Yeah, grand, chat ya in a while.' He walks back into his room.

I am starving, I cut up tomatoes and ham and put them on the toast, take crips from the press and a bottle of water and sit and eat. The door bangs, that's Conor back. He comes into the kitchen, puts the kettle on and the two of us sit down and talk. He's pestering me about tonight, but I pass no remarks. He soon stops, and we talk about other things.

'Jeez, there's a lot of cars here.'

'Yeah, I know,' says Tom. 'Oh there, a car is pulling out.'

'Great, that worked out well.' I turn into the spot and head in.

I drove because I was not in the mood for a drink after our wild night out. Think it will take me a few weeks before I drink again.

We walk in and there's a sign that says *wait to be seated*.

The maitre d comes over. 'Hi, what's the name?'

'*Ah*, Coen, for four.'

She looks at her book. '*Ah* yes, follow me.'

We follow her to the table and Megan is there before us. I slyly look at my watch, it's only 8.11. Megan is very punctual.

She sees us approaching and stands. She obviously gives Tom a kiss and me a hug.

The three of us sit.

'So, Ciaran, how are you? Haven't chatted to you in a while.'

I pour the bottle of water that must have been placed when Megan came into our glasses.

'I know, the time is flying. I can't believe it's been like what two months since I saw you. Well, obviously, apart from the other night, but I drank a lot that night so this is a proper catch up.'

'You were fine because we all drank a lot that night. When I was looking at the photos, I was like oh lord we all look so drunk, but it was a fun night. So, is Tara coming or has she something to do?'

'No, she's coming, said she had to work till seven.' I feel like saying, you know as much as I do where Tara is. Why is it that when a person is casually seeing someone, other people ask where they are and implying we should know. Everything is always 'Oh where's the woman or man you are seeing?' We are not stuck to one another.

As if on cue, Megan puts her head up and waves, I know it's Tara, but I turn anyway and smile at her. She smiles at us all; we all stand when she comes over. I put my hand on her waist and kiss her on the cheek. 'Hey, Tara.' I'm sure Megan is looking at us like we are so cute. Oh, I hate that crap.

'Hey, Tara,' both Tom and Megan say.

'Hi, Guys,' Tara replies, and we all sit.

'Sorry, I'm late, I got a flat tyre, so my brother dropped me off there.'

OK, I have to be the nice boyfriend here and say what Tom and Megan are expecting me to say. '*Awh*, you should have rung me, I would have collected you.'

She pats my shoulder. 'No it's fine, Mike owed me a favour

anyway.' She has a look that implies she doesn't want to say any more, but we are all looking at her waiting. 'OK, it's nothing, I'm sure ye two both know anyway.' She gestures to Megan and Tom and looks at me. 'Rachel thought she was pregnant and she had an appointment with gynae, so Mike couldn't bring her and asked me, but it turned out she wasn't pregnant so she was, I suppose, disappointed. So, I brought her to a spa for some pampering. She just needed encouragement that they would get pregnant, and she shouldn't put so much pressure on herself. So, Mike told me later it helped. So, the least he could do was give me a lift here, *ha-ha*, and collect me too.'

I take a sip of my water. 'Tara, I can bring you home, text your brother there and let him know.'

'No, Ciaran, honestly it's fine.' She puts her bag on the ground.

'No, Tara, I won't take no for an answer. Text Mike there.'

She looks at me and bites her lip.

'I mean it. Text him.'

'Okay, are you sure?'

'Yeah, of course.' I can feel Megan beam with how cute we are. As Tara takes out her phone to text Mike, I look across the table at Megan and Tom and roll my eyes at their obvious joyful expressions. This is so embarrassing and irritating. Feck's sake, it's a lift home, not a marriage proposal. But I can't complain too much because it makes me look good.

The conversation flows among the four of us while we have dinner and dessert. Tom and I being the kind gentlemen pay for the dinner. We are now ending the night with a few drinks at the bar. I bought the first round because it's the only drink I will be having.

I don't know how, but we have end up talking about the

drunken night last week.

'Oh, they were so funny, Tara. They went up chatting to two lads and pretended they were children of Roy Keane. So, they were asking what he was like at home; he is great and easy going and secretly a Liverpool fan. Their faces dropped. Then they asked Tom and Ciaran if they knew the story of their parents' first date. They just looked at each other and made some story, but the lads mentioned the Tommy Tiernan interview and oh my god, they started stuttering and looking around, then the lads figured it out. One of them said, "I knew he would never support Liverpool," and he looked at Ciaran and followed by saying, "You had me thinking he did, not cool".'

My head is hung in shame because it's kind of coming back to me. Tara is bursting laughing and Megan has to stop to laugh. Tom is in stitches.

'Anyway, we had to go to another pub after that.' She puts her hands out and says, 'And I never told ye, but they were in that pub and saw ye and left, *ha-ha*.' She puts her hand on her chest, laughing.

'Oh my god, yeah it's slowly coming back to me.' I put my finger to my lip, trying to think if anything else comes back.

'Did we do shots with a girl because we thought she looked like Miley Cyrus?'

Megan takes a sip of her drink and then her hand goes out 'Yeah! You paid for the round and wanted a photo. Oh crap, who took that photo? It might have been Jen; I'll ask her and get her to send it to me.'

Tom looks at me and Megan, puts his hand through his hair and says, 'What the heck were we at? You would swear we were never out before. I blame the shots.'

I don't know if this is making Tara turn off from me or if she thinks it's all hilarious. She finally chimes in, 'Oh lord, hopefully, Roy Keane won't message and give you a TAKEN monologue.' She laughs while taking a drink.

I look at her. 'I know, right? I'm not out of the woods yet, he could still call. I'll give it a month before I can breathe properly!'

And you, Tara, you poor naïve woman will not be talking to me in a month.

'Oh, that reminds me, that photo you wanted taken with my friends of them kissing you on the cheek...' Megan looks at Tom. *What? Tom wanted that photo?*

'What?' I say. 'Tom wanted that photo taken.'

Megan looks at me, confused. 'Yeah, and then you wanted one too.' She looks at Tara.

Tom and I look at each other and Tom asks before I get a chance, 'But where is that photo?'

'Oh, it's on my phone. Here, I'll show you, we didn't put it up because you looked passed out so...' She roots in her bag and takes out her phone. 'Now where is it, *ah*, here it is' and gives Tom her phone. 'Oh lord, yeah, I look like I'm asleep.'

'Here, show.' He gives me the phone to look and Tara and I burst laughing. 'Yeah you really do, maybe you did fall asleep. Poor baby was tired,' I mock with a soothing tone.

Tom has his head in his hands and looks at Megan. 'Thank you for not putting that up.'

Megan puts her hand to her chest. '*Awh*, I didn't have the heart to do that to my baby.' She teases to support me and then says, 'But I did for Ciaran, *ha*, yours is so funny.' She shows the three of us the photo giggling as she waves the phone around the table. She takes back the phone and puts it in her bag. 'Ah, it's so funny.' She then looks at Tara. 'But don't worry, Tara, he didn't cheat.'

Oh, crap! She had to say it, change the subject. I look at Tom, or should I say glare at Tom.

He understands and says, 'One more round for the road? Same again for everyone?' He looks at us all and we agree. I kindly offer to go up and bring the drinks down to the table with Tom.

'*Phew*, thanks for that, mate.'

'Yeah, worked out that my drink was gone.'

'Yeah, I hope that's the end of it now.' We both exhale, and Tom holds his card out to pay for the drinks.

We bring the drinks down to the table. Tara and Megan thank us. 'But yeah, anyway, as I was saying before being interrupted' – Megan looks at me and Tom – 'the photo of Tom and my friends, well, Jen photoshopped Tom Cruise into it and showed people from work the photo and told them we just bumped into him and approached for this kind of photo, and he said yes.'

'What, really?' Tara asks.

'Yeah, they all believed it.' Megan grins at us all.

'Do you have that photo?' Tara asks again.

'No, she has it on her phone but didn't want to put it on social media in case someone saw, or Tom Cruise saw and next thing we're making headlines for faking the photo and defamation or something like that. But it looks so cool, the face shape and everything, so accurate.'

Thankfully, that's where the conversation topic remains along with work problems, holidays and the weather. Time to go when the weather chat started.

The three of us are in the car, Tom lets Tara sit in the front. I drop Tom home first. 'Nice seeing you again, Tara, and, Ciaran, if you get delayed, just give me a text.' He winks at me and says, 'Bye.'

The prick! 'Sorry about Tom,' I say as I pull out of the parking lane.

Tara waves her hand. 'Don't worry about it, I'm sorry about what Megan said.'

'What do you mean?'

'You know, about cheating; I don't want either one of us to feel pressured, like we haven't had that conversation and I think we are happy enough with no labels being put on ourselves. Right?'

Crap, what do I say here? If I agree with her, it will dampen our situation and I will prove to her right that I'm not a changed man, but if I don't agree and hint at making this serious, she might get scared and end things. Either way, I'm screwed, and I have to make my mind up now! *Damn you, Megan!*

'Well, what if we don't have labels but are getting close to having the labels, would that be OK?' I had to say something to hint I cared and did not want to run. Thankfully, I have to watch the road because there's a car turning off; this helps me avoid looking at her while she makes her mind up. Finally, she answers, 'Yeah, that could work.'

I look at her shocked because I genuinely am. 'Really?'

She smiles at me. 'Yeah.'

'Ah, OK, then, great.' I don't know why, but I start humming the theme tune to Friends. *What the heck is wrong with me?*

Tara joins in, singing, 'I'll be there for you...'

We both mischievously laugh as I pull outside her place.

She has her hand on the door handle, turns her head and asks, 'Do you want to come in?'

Better make this official. 'Yeah, sure.' I smile at her, and we both get out of the car.

Chapter Fifteen

It's been a busy two weeks; I barely saw the lads and if Tom and I didn't get up around the same time in the morning, I'd never see him either. I've seen Tara once and she was working. The school is due an inspection, so the principal is rigorous and annoyingly checking that everything looks appropriate for the inspection. Don't know why she is so stringent; her husband works for the department so if that isn't a benefit, then I don't know what is.

The nonsense they want done, copybooks have to be checked, reports written up, posters hanging and timetables done. The posters have to follow a specific structure and visual. I bought one online but it looked like the bear was crouching to go to the bathroom, so I don't think that would follow the specifics the department is looking for.

My phone is ringing. *Crap! Where did I put it?* Ah yes, it's in my coat pocket. I pull over the car and get out, open the back passenger door, and take it out of the pocket. Oh, a missed call from Tara. I ring her back.

'Hey, Ciaran.'

'Hey, Tara, sorry I missed your call.'

'It's grand, I thought it would be safe to ring now because school is finished, but does it suit you to chat?'

'Yeah, I'm just heading into the shop to buy food.'

'Sorry, I can call you later'.

'No, it's fine, honestly.' *Get to the point, please.*

'Okay, my dad rang me, and he and my mother were going away this weekend...' Oh, now where is this leading, do we have to babysit children, animals? Do we have to meet them somewhere with the rest of the family? That's too much for me. Oh no, I tuned out, what did she say? 'So, anyway, they wanted to know if we wanted them?'

Wanted them? Tickets? Vouchers?

'Ciaran?'

'Yeah, sorry, the phone fell on the ground, yeah sure.'

'Really? You want to go?'

'Yeah sure, when is it?' I close my eyes as I ask, afraid she'll get mad for asking again.

'It's booked for this Friday. Dad said it's dinner, concert and breakfast in the morning.'

Okay, so it sounds like it's a night away. I can do that. Wish I didn't trail off now because I don't know why he offered them to us. I'll find out eventually and hopefully in a subtle way. 'Yeah, Friday suits me. What time?'

'Yeah, so, dinner is booked for seven, so leave around five.'

'OK, cool. Can you send me a link to the place or the postcode?' I'm assuming it has to be an hour away.

'Yeah, I'll send it to you now.' I can hear tapping on her side. 'OK, sent.'

I look at the message. Wow, it looks nice. 'Wow, it's very nice.' I quickly type it in my maps. Forty minutes away, that's fine.

'OK, I'll pick you up at five. At your place or the café?'

'*Ah*, the café is fine, I don't mind driving.'

'Nonsense, you can drive the next time,' I say, and I am cringing now. Crap, didn't mean to get her hopes up, Oh well.

I can hear her smiling on the phone with excitement. 'OK, great. I'll see you at five on Friday. Bye.'

'Bye, Tara.'

I arrive back with my shopping; I hear the door close and it's Conor. I nearly didn't recognise him because his hair has grown; normally, he's a stickler for keeping it tight.

'Hey, man, you look different with your hair.' I look at him as I says it.

Conor touches it. 'Oh, yeah, I thought I'd let it grow a bit more, hard to keep it tight. Sure, I was going to the barber's once a week, it's too much really.'

'*Hmmm.*'

'What?'

'That's not the reason.' I fold my arms, waiting for an explanation.

'OK, I've been seeing someone casually, and then for the last two weeks I was seeing more of her.'

'Ah no way!' I tap him on the shoulder. 'And I was feeling bad that I didn't see you, thought it was because I was staying longer at school. So, where did you meet her? Online?'

'Obviously online. I work with men and I live with men, where would I meet a woman?'

'Yeah, suppose, so the hair?'

'Yeah, she said she never saw it grow and asked about it one night, so I said I get it cut once a week. So, she convinced me to let it grow a bit and see what it's like, so what do you think?'

'Yeah, it is nice, just getting used to it but yeah, makes you look mature.'

'*Ha-ha*, thanks.'

'So, what's her name?'

'Rhona.'

'*Ah* right, well, that's great, nice you met someone.'

'Yeah, it's weird, didn't think I'd like someone this quick, like spending so much time with the same person.'

I put the milk in the fridge and the biscuits in the press as I listen.

'Yeah, I know, sure. I'm going for a night away this Friday,' I say as I close the press. I shut my eyes before I face him. Crap, that kind of slipped out; we were bonding and I forgot myself.

'*OOOH*. Very nice, was it you or her that booked it?'

'She didn't book it; something happened with her dad and he offered them to her.'

'Sure.' He puts water in the kettle and flicks on the switch.

'It did!'

'Oh yeah. What?'

'I don't know, I didn't hear properly because I was freaking out while she was talking.'

'Sounds to me things are getting serious.'

'No, it's just a gesture.' I hope.

'Do you want coffee?'

'Yeah, get a sachet there.'

'So, did you tell Tom?'

He puts a teabag into a cup and a sachet of cappuccino into another.

'No, I just got off the phone with her. Oh, Tom is going to wreck my head about it.'

'Yeah, he's such a romantic. That lad.'

'Yeah, makes me sick.'

I'm all packed and on the way to collect Tara. The contents in my case are literally a pants and shirt and I will be wearing the same thing I have on today, tomorrow. I have never heard of the singer we are going to listen to, but I listened to one of his songs on YouTube and he sounds pretty good.

Tara is waiting outside the café with a small suitcase. If that is packed with outfits, I will be puzzled. I mean how many items of clothes would a person need for one night?

I get out of the car and greet her with a kiss.

'Hey, I'll take your suitcase.'

'*Awh*, thanks, Ciaran.' She opens the passenger door and hops in. I probably should have opened the door for her, but I can't be doing everything at once. Anyway, I don't think she minds. The suitcase is light, so she didn't overload it anyway.

I get into the car and reach for my seatbelt. 'The suitcase was a good idea, easier to carry than a gear bag.'

'Yeah, I only used the suitcase because I didn't have room for my shoes in a big handbag I was initially going to bring. At least the clothes aren't crumpled together in the suitcase.'

'Yeah, that's true, you can see what you want.'

'Yes, exactly,' she says enthusiastically.

We arrive at the Spring Lodge in under forty minutes, the road was surprisingly quiet. There's a fountain outside it and a big Gothic-style entrance.

'My father said there's parking around the back.'

I still haven't asked why we got the tickets, but I'm hoping Tara will mention it again.

We park and walk into the front entrance. I obviously and chivalrously carry Tara's suitcase. We book in and head for the elevator.

'Ciaran?'

I turn and see a brown-haired woman wearing a black dress. It takes me a second to know who it is.

'Oh, sorry. Hey, Zoe, took me a minute. You changed your

hair.'

She touches it. 'Yeah, I did, so how are you?' She looks at me and then at Tara.

'Yeah, I'm good.' I get the hint. 'Sorry.' I turn to Tara. 'This is Tara; Tara, this is Zoe.'

Tara steps forward. 'Hi, Zoe, nice to meet you.'

Zoe responds, 'Yeah, you too.'

'So, what are you doing here?' I ask.

'Well, my sister is forty, so we are just having dinner and a few drinks to mark it. How about ye?' She looks at the both of us.

I'm about to answer but Tara speaks before me. 'My father got tickets and booked this hotel for his and my mother's anniversary, but he got the bad flu two days ago. So, he knew he wouldn't be feeling better for the trip. No real point in going anywhere when you feel bad, so he offered them to me and Ciaran.' She looks at me as she says my name. I look at her and smile and I look at Zoe. I can see the bewilderment in her face. Great, now I know why we are here.

'Oh yeah, I saw the signs for the concert. How's your dad feeling now? There's a lot of bad bugs going around.'

'He's still the same, coughing a lot and tired. It'll take another few days before he feels better.'

Oh my god! Tara must think I'm a complete ass for not asking about her dad.

'Well, nice to see you and Ciaran and very nice to meet you, Tara.' She smiles at us both and heads outside. She looks back one more time at me and smiles. Whatever that means.

We head up to the room and start to take our clothes out. 'So, who was Zoe? An ex?' Tara asks as she takes her dress out of her suitcase.

I should have said it to her straight away. I turn to face her after taking my shirt out and putting it on a hanger.

'Ah well, kind of, not really. We saw each other briefly for about a month. She was subbing at the school, so we got together a few times while she was there. I know, not my proudest moment, because we saw each other in a professional setting. But anyway, then she got a job somewhere else and to be honest, it suited me, so I kind of let it be known that it was fun and moved on and I haven't seen her since.' I put my hands in my pockets. 'Yeah, so that was awkward.'

'So, did she take it well, to move on?'

'*Ah*, she did because she had a boyfriend.'

Tara puts her hand to her mouth in shock.

'Yeah, like I said, not my proudest moment.'

'*Hmm*, wonder if she's still with him?'

I click my fingers. 'Damn, should've asked her.'

'Yeah' – Tara laughs – 'next time you see her.'

'Yeah, must write it down.'

'So, was that long ago?' She continues to take clothes out of her suitcase.

'*Ah*, about a year ago, I think.'

'Right and no new subs in your school?'

'No, just two younger lads. Come to think of it, that could be for my benefit.' I laugh awkwardly, hoping she will too, and she does. *Phew!*

'Did anyone know about ye?'

'Ah, I don't think so. No one ever said anything to me, maybe a bit of flirting, but that was all anyone would have noticed. Honestly, Tara, it feels like a lifetime ago.' I know I should go over to her and hold her hand or kiss her, but I feel she'd believe me more if remain where I am.

'Yeah, I know, Ciaran, everyone has a past, especially men. Anyway, I'm just going to go shower.' She walks past me and puts her hand on my waist, and I hold my hand there too.

The two of us are finishing up getting ready, I watched TV while Tara had a shower. Then when she was finished, I had a quick shower and put on my clothes, so I was more or less ready, just had to admire myself one last time in the mirror. Tara surprisingly didn't take too long to do her hair and makeup. She is still in the bathroom doing the final touches.

'Sorry, Ciaran, will you just finish zipping me up?'

I plug my phone out and say, 'Yeah.' I go over and zip her up. She turns around and fixes her dress.

'Now I'm ready,' Tara says, smiling at me.

'Wow.' I exhale. 'You look beautiful.' She does; her dress is black and tight but not stuck to her. Her hair is pinned up and it all makes her look so classy.

'*Awh*. Thanks, Ciaran.' She brushes some lint off her dress. 'You don't look too bad yourself.'

'Well, thank you. Actually, I just want to use the mirror and then I'm ready.'

'Oh, men, ye take forever to get ready,' Tara says cheekily.

We get to our table and the place is so busy. I look around to see where the fortieth birthday is, but I don't see any balloon. It must be held in the function room. We finish our meal and polish off our wine glasses. I'm not normally a fan of wine, but it tastes nice.

People are starting to head into the venue, 'Do you want to head in now?' I ask. 'Or do you want to have another drink?'

Tara looks at her glass. '*Ah*, no, let's head in now.'

We both finish our drinks and head towards the venue. And of course, we bump into Zoe and another woman. 'Hey, Ciaran; hey, Tara.'

'Hey, Zoe, we meet again,' I say.

'Yeah,' and then she looks at the woman with her. 'Oh sorry, this is my sister Erin,' she whispers, then saying, 'it's her fortieth.'

'Oh, happy birthday,' Tara says.

Probably should say it too and then we can move on. 'Happy birthday, definitely don't look forty.'

Erin thanks me.

'Oh, Ciaran, always the flatterer,' Zoe chimes. 'Keep an eye on him, Tara.'

Tara takes my hand. 'Oh, I will' and smiles.

Zoe smiles at us and then looks at Erin. 'Well, we better go, nice seeing you two again.'

'Nice meeting ye,' says Erin.

'Yeah, you too,' Tara answers and I finish with 'Bye, enjoy your night.'

Thank Christ that's over. What were the chances I would meet her again so soon? Why didn't we stay for another drink?

Tara and I remain still for a moment. I look at her. 'Shall we?' And gesture towards the venue.

'Yeah.' We show our tickets and get a seat in the middle. 'I'm sorry, Tara, again about Zoe.'

She bats her hand. 'It's fine, Ciaran, but I think she still is hung up on you.'

I look at her. 'What?'

'Oh yeah, I could see it in her eyes. It was like jealousy, but also desire.'

'You could tell all that in a few awkward minutes and

conversation?'

'Yeah, women just know, we see things ye are oblivious to.'

'*Hmph*. I never asked if she had a boyfriend. Damn.'

'Well, if she had, she would dump him in that moment if she thought she had a chance with you.'

'OK, genius, did she think she had a chance in that conversation?' I say with air quotes.

'*Ammm,* no, I don't think so.' She bumps me gently on the shoulder, smiles and faces towards the stage.

Well, she's right there because I never had any interest in her, it was just entertainment for me. The lights go down and the concert begins.

The concert was very enjoyable, he was very charismatic and entertaining. He really got the audience off their feet. I would go as far as saying I would go to his concert again.

After the concert, he comes down to meet the audience. Tara looks at me. 'Do you want a photo?'

'Oh, yeah, definitely!'

'OK, let's go up.'

'Wait what? I wasn't being serious.'

'*Awh*, come on, just to have it. My parents might need proof we went to this; what more proof would they need, only a picture from the man himself?' She gestures towards the stage.

I'm all for attending concerts but a photo especially when she looks at it in two weeks' time will rip it apart. But I can't refuse, that will cause an argument.

'OK, fine, one photo.' I hold up one finger.

'Yes, yes, come on.' She grabs my hand, and we walk over to Mike Harris.

We are in the front bar having another few night caps. It was supposed to be one, but we got chatting to other people who went to the concert. Tara is going through her photos, we ended up taking more than one and multiple options. There was one of the three of us, one of me and Tara (weirdly, Mike offered to take that), one of just me and Mike and then one of Tara and Mike. She shows me the one of us two again.

'It's nice, isn't it?'

I look at it again. 'Yeah, it is.'

'Do you want me to send it to you?'

'Oh yeah, do, of course.' This puts a smile on her face as wide as the bar. Glad that pleased her.

We get back to our room and can't keep our hands off each other. I trip over my bag as we walk to the bed and bang my leg. I have to stop kissing Tara. 'Ouch.'

'Oh, are you OK?'

I sit on the bed and wait for the pain to subside before I answer. 'Yeah I'm OK now, come here.'

She does so willingly. She puts each knee on either side of my waist and continues to kiss me. We lie back on the bed; I start to unzip her dress and then my hand moves to her ass, and I squeeze it hard with the intensity. Tara smiles as we continue to kiss. She gets off me slowly unzips the rest of her dress and lowers it slowly off her shoulders, arms and body. She kicks it to one side of the room; I can't not stare in fascination as she undresses. She stands there in her black bra and underwear and motions me to sit up, I do as I'm told. She repositions herself on my lap and as we continue to kiss, she unbuttons my shirt. I grab her by the waist and lay her on the bed. I undo my belt and take off my pants, we stare at each other as I do it. I walk over to the end of the bed, put my arms on her legs and slowly slide her down to me. I kiss her ankle then make my way up towards her thigh, I grip her underwear and gently roll it down her legs. I put my finger inside her and then two, she groans loudly, she is so wet. I pull her legs closer to me and kneel, I kiss her inner thigh left and right, I put my mouth inside her and circle my tongue around her clit. She breaths heavily and then her breathing quickens. It feels good to her gasp for breath. When her breathing slows down, I remove my boxers, lay her back on the bed and slide into her, gently at first and then quickly and hard the next time. Her breathing is slow at first and then quickens with our pace. I cannot hold it any longer. *AHHHH!* I let go. She groans with pleasure, and I join her. I roll off her and we catch our breath.

I look at her and between breaths, say, 'That was fun.'

'Yeah, so is there a bit more stamina in you?'

I look at her, puzzled. '*Ah*, yeah, I think so.'

She smiles. 'Good.'

'Why?' I ask. She says nothing and slides down the bed to give me a happy ending.

We go down for breakfast the next morning and I can't help yawning; between the drinking and the pleasuring, it really has taken the energy out of me.

Tara brings her fry over to the table; she catches me yawning. '*Awh*, are you tired?'

'What? No! I don't know why I keep yawning.'

'Old age, Ciaran, can't handle the late nights the way you used to.'

'*Ha-ha*, yeah, probably all the energy I used during the concert.'

'Yeah, that's probably it. Anyway, it's early yet, we can always go to bed for a while, and I mean that the old-fashioned way.'

'Sad to say, but I might.'

'Yeah fine, well finish eating and head up. I'll set my alarm for about half ten. Does that work?'

'Yeah, great. I'll set mine too.' We finish eating and head back up to our room.

I wake up and roll over to Tara, I put my arm around her waist and pull her towards me. 'Oh, I feel so much better after that sleep.'

'*Hmm,* yeah, me too.'

We get up and out of bed and Tara twists her back from side to side. 'Hey, are you OK?'

'Yeah, just my back is a bit sore, and my chest feels a bit heavy.'

'Well, hey, I have Panadol in my bag. Do you want to take one or two?'

'Yeah, I'll take one, might just need to do a few stretches later. Probably just muscle tightness.'

'Look, sit there and I'll pack your suitcase and my bag and then we'll head off.'

'Yeah, great, thanks, Ciaran.'

'So, do you have to go into the café today?'

'Yeah, I'll go in at around three and I'll close up, the pain should be eased off by then.'

We leave the hotel before twelve and I drop Tara at her house. I take the suitcase out of the car and carry it to her door. 'So, call me if you need help in the café and just send me a text when the pain eases.'

'I will, don't worry, I'll be fine. Thanks for caring though.' She kisses me on the lips. 'I'll chat you later. Bye.'

I kiss her one more time and smile, saying, 'Bye.'

Chapter Sixteen

I get back home and head straight for the bed. I'm so tired. I wake to a horn beeping outside; I look out the window and it's one of our neighbours beeping for his wife (I'm assuming) to come out of the house. For feck's sake, why can't she just come out already; the ripple effect of her not coming out on time has disturbed my sleep and I'm sure other people are pissed to be listening to a horn. Some people are so self-centred!

Well, I'm up now, may as well eat something. I go into the kitchen and Tom and Conor are there.

They look away from the TV when they see me. 'Hey, mate, how was your night with Tara? Did you propose?' Conor says with a wide smile.

I open the fridge door and say, 'Feck off, yeah, it was good.' I take ham and cheese out of the fridge and put bread in the toaster.

'Are you sick?' Tom asks.

I fill the kettle with water and ask, 'What? Oh no, just tired, do any of ye want tea or something?'

'Yeah, make me tea will ya, please?' Conor asks. 'Yeah, grand.'

'So, do you think you'll be able for tomorrow night?' asks Tom.

I put the kettle on the boil, turn and ask, 'What's tomorrow night?'

'You know, Gavin's stag.'

'What? Is that tomorrow night?'

'Yeah, the bank holiday.'

'Jeez, I completely forgot about that.' I put my hand to my head. 'Yeah, I'll be fine for it, but I won't drink much. What time are we going at?'

'Around half one, the meal is at five and then the match and I think we are staying in the bar then. He just wants to mark it, nothing huge or elaborate.'

'Yeah, he was always like that, even when he was staying here. Sure, he never told any of us about his promotion or his birthday either and you should have known, he's your cousin.'

'*Ah* come on, I can't remember all my cousins' birthday. Do you know all yours?'

'No. Not one, actually.' I continue to make my sandwich and make tea for Conor and coffee for me. I bring them over to the table and then go back for my sandwich.

'Hey, where's my sandwich?' Conor asks.

I'm about to eat my sandwich and then look at Conor and say, 'Yeah, sorry, all my considerate coupons are used up for the day. Try again tomorrow.' I smile at Conor and continue to eat my sandwich.

I'm hungover and tired and the prick wants me to make him a sandwich, he can feck off!

We watch some teen comedy film and then I head to my bed to sleep off the last of this hangover.

We get up early and Conor cooks us a fry; it's the one meal he can cook with confidence without fear of burning. Me and Tom sit at the table and Conor brings over the plates.

'We'll be full for the day after this,' Conor says.

'Yeah, thanks, Mum,' I say cheekily.

Tom joins in, saying, 'Yeah, Mum, you're the greatest.'

'Feck off, ye can get your own food now.' He comes over to the table with his plate.

'Ah, Ma, that's not fair,' Tom argues mockingly.

'Up, the two of ye, and get it; as J Lo says, I ain't your mama.'

'You keep talking like that and you'll be more like our grandmother,' I say laughing as me and Tom get up to obtain our food.

It was a good idea to have the fry as we have been driving for forty minutes and I feel a bit peckish; if I didn't eat the fry, I think my stomach would be making some noise now.

I send a quick message to Tara to tell her about the stag in case she sees photos online.

Hey Tara, Tom's cousin is having his stag tonight (I completely forgot it was on) so just to warn you in case you get a few drunken texts! Sorry in advance.

'Texting the missus?' Conor asks.

'*Ha ha*, I am, just in case one of ye takes my phone and texts her. She'll know in advance it isn't me. Also, I forgot about this stag; so, if she sees photos online, she might think I purposely didn't tell her. Keeps me out of trouble.'

'Right, so best behaviour.'

'Well, we'll see,' I reply with a glint in my eye. I'll be single again soon, so no harm to have one ready.

She texts back with a thumbs up.

'Right, so you are still keeping it casual?'

'*Hmm?* Oh yeah, well, like if I find someone better, I'll call it off, but so far, I haven't, so keeping things the way they are.'

'Wow, you should really write for Hallmark, I can see the

card now.' He puts his hand in front and moves it from left to right. 'To my lovely girlfriend, well, until someone better comes along. You won't even need a tender message inside the card.'

'Yeah, well, the joke will be on you when the card gets sold out due to high demand.'

By the time all the men attend the meal, it is past five o'clock. The match is starting at half seven and it's a twenty-minute walk. We all get our meal at quarter to six. There's not much time to sit and talk after it. So, we had a few drinks while we waited for the meal and during the meal. We get to the bar at quarter past seven. Poor Gavin was so anxious to get there before the match started that it wasn't until we got our seats at the bar did he finally relax. His team won so he was probably happier about the win than if it were his wedding day. There has been a smile on his face all night. I'm about to head outside because it is so hot in the bar and a woman approaches me. She looks familiar.

'Hey, Ciaran.'

'Hey... Ciara?' Really not sure if that's the right name.

'Kara,' she retorts. Right, not her name, but close enough. 'Wow, you really haven't changed.'

'What? What do you mean?'

'Not remembering my name, not even caring that you don't remember, same old Ciaran.' She puts a piece of her hair behind her ear.

'No, sorry, I'm just on a stag, so I'm distracted. A lot of names I have had to remember tonight.'

'Oh, nice save there, I almost believe it.'

I don't get it, she's obviously annoyed but still remains standing to talk to me.

'Yeah, a bit of a lame excuse, apologies. So, how are you?'

Moving on quickly to her because I'm sure she'll want to talk about herself. It will be a nice break from her clever comments.

'Yeah, good, I am the vice principal at St Enda's school. It's about an hour's drive from here.'

Oh yes, now I remember her; we met at a teaching conference. I had to represent the school because Joe who was the secretary of some association got sick, so I had to go. Why did I go again? Oh yes, now I remember. I was subbing at the time and wanted to get ahead of the other subs, and it gave me a better chance of getting the permanent job that was on offer.

'Oh great, good for you. So, you're busy with it?' Not that I care one bit.

'Yeah, kept busy, I teach and then have a lot of paperwork because it's a big school.'

Yeah, yeah, I get it, you are very much accomplished in your field of work. But I would not care if you were the president of the country, you're way too boring for me. Jeez woman, it was a few dates along with other things, don't need to impress me because I don't care.

'Right well, it's great to be kept busy anyway,' I reply. I'm about to walk away but she has other ideas because she starts another conversation.

'So, how have you been?'

'*Ah* yeah, good, like I said, I'm just on a stag.'

'Oh, is it your own?'

I hope she's not serious. 'Oh no, definitely not.'

'Yeah, I thought that but wasn't sure.'

'No, it's a guy I used to live with.'

'Oh right. So, are you seeing anyone?' This is weird. Why is she asking me this?

'Yeah, casually seeing someone. How about you?' Not that

I care.

'Yeah, I am, his name is Andrew…' Didn't ask. 'He's in New York this week for a conference.'

Zoned out when she said his job. 'Right, is he doing any sightseeing while he's out there or is it a flying visit?' Really don't care, but I better ask something.

'It's a flying visit, his conference finishes at one on Thursday and he's booked on the flight at half four. Hopefully, next time it can be incorporated as a holiday.'

'Yeah, I was there once, it's a great city.'

'Oh really? I'll have to pick your brain on where to go.' Why would I be talking to her after tonight? She takes a sip of her drink and looks at me.

Is she flirting with me? This is weird.

'Yeah. Sure. Anyway, I better get back to the lads before they send out a search, I'll chat ya again.'

'Yeah, see you, Ciaran,' she says.

I head back to the lads; I feel her eyes are on me. What was that about? She has a boyfriend and doesn't like me.

Gavin greets me back to the group. 'Hey, who was that you were talking to?'

I take a sip of my drink. 'Oh, that is Kara, we were kind of seeing each other a while back.'

'Well, it seems she still likes you.' He darts his eyes behind my head. 'She's looking over at you.'

'What? Really?'

'Yeah, she's turned now, and it looks like she's going over to two other women.'

'Yeah, it was weird she saw me and was coarse towards me and then all of a sudden it felt like she was flirting with me, and she said she had a boyfriend, weird.'

'Maybe she's one of those women where when you treat them mean and they are always keen.'

'Yeah, it definitely seems that way, like I was barely listening to her.'

'*Ha-ha*, anyway, come on, we're doing one round of shots to toast my wedding and being glad I never have to deal with any of that kind of foolishness again.'

'Oh, give it time and you'll miss it.'

'*Hmm*, maybe, but not at the moment.'

The shot went straight to my head, I think it went to everyone's head. I get a glass of water from the bar and head to the bathroom. When I come out and the band has started playing, I'm walking over to the lads when I bump into Kara again. I hope it's a coincidence that I would see her again in less than an hour and not purposely done on her part.

'Hey, Ciaran, we meet again.'

'Hey, Kara. Yeah, I know,' I say with humour.

'I hope it's not a ploy of yours just to get chatting to me again!' She giggles.

'What?' I ask, confused. 'No, I was just going to the bathroom.' *WTF?* If anything, it's a ploy on her side because the women's toilets are on the other side; there is actually nothing on this side, only the men's bathroom.

'Relax, Ciaran, I'm messing.'

'Oh, right, *ha!*' So funny, even though I know it was a ploy on your side.

'So, which one of your friends is getting married?'

I turn to show her. 'It's the guy in the blue and white shirt.'

'Oh, right and when is he getting married?' she says into my ear.

'*Ah*, the 22nd—'

'Sorry, Ciaran, I can't hear you. Will we pop outside to chat?'

Chat? This isn't a chat, it's mindless conversation that can be finished now. But OK, I better say yes.

'Yeah, fine,' I say.

We go outside and I finish saying, 'Yeah so, the 22nd of—'

She turns into me and says, 'Ciaran. I have to say it's good to see you.'

'Yeah, you too.' She goes to kiss me, I back away. '*Whooo*, what is this? You have a boyfriend.'

'Oh, don't act like that bothers you.' She steps towards me again.

'Kara! What the fuck?' I yell.

'Jeez, Ciaran, you don't do boring, and you don't do frisky, starting to feel it's me you didn't like.'

'Look, Kara, you were great' – *bit boring for me* – 'you are great, but I'm on a stag, and it wouldn't be right leaving my friends to go off with a woman for the night. Also, the lads would kill me so I don't want that.'

'A woman?'

'Well, you are a woman, Kara, so that's what I mean. I can't just go off and leave my friend's stag.'

'Or maybe this woman is changing you.'

'No, it's not that, it's just there's a time and place for this carry-on and it's not at my friend's stag and maybe you are acting this way because you are missing Andrew or trying to sabotage the relationship because you don't want to be in it.'

'Wow, when did you get so deep?'

'It's not me being deep, it's just that I have heard it a lot.'

There's silence. 'Look, Kara, I wish you well. Are you going to be OK?'

'*Hm?* Yeah, I'm fine, thanks.'

'OK, I better head in. Are you coming?'

She gives a brief smile. 'Yeah, better find my friends, think I have drunk too much, time to go.'

'OK, come on.' I gesture for her to follow.

She sees her friends and turns to me and gives me a hug. 'See you, Ciaran.'

'Yeah. Bye, Kara.'

I exhale as I head back to the lads. I stand beside Tom and he says, 'Hey, I saw you head outside with a woman, Gavin said you knew her.'

'Yeah, we briefly dated, and she just tried to kiss me.'

'What?' Tom steps back in shock. '*Whoo*, you must have briefly rocked her world.'

All the lads hear Tom roaring *whoo*, I look to see if Kara is around, but she's not. *Phew!*

'Hey, hey, hey, this is Gavin's stag. Keep it in your pants tonight, Ciaran,' Conor teases as he takes a drink.

'I'm trying but what can I do when I'm this good looking?' I shrug as I say it, looking for sympathy.

'Yeah, yeah, yeah, so where is she?' Gavin asks.

'Ah, I don't know. I assume she went off with her friends, probably left after the rejection.'

'Did she know you were casually seeing someone?

'Yeah, I told her, and she said she had a boyfriend, he's in New York on business.'

'Wow, you match. Do you have her number?'

'No, I deleted it ages ago. Why?'

'Well, she's not into commitment obviously, so she's perfect for you. There's no pressure, so why not?'

Tom chimes in, 'Or maybe she *was* perfect for him.'

I turn to Tom, confused. 'What? Was?'

'Yeah was, as in not now.'

'Why would you say that?' I ask.

'Well, you've been seeing Tara a lot,' Tom remarks.

'Yeah, but me and Tara are just casual,' I say defensively.

'You know where casual leads,' Gavin joins in.

'Yeah, eventually fizzling out,' I retort.

'No, casual leads to serious!' He says it louder so I would understand what he is implying.

'No way!'

'*Hmm*, normally, it does; you have already refused a woman tonight.' Gavin smirks.

'Because there is a time and place and my friend's stag is not the time or the place for that. Maybe the next night though.'

'I don't think you will,' Gavin says.

'What? Why?' I ask.

Gavin continues, 'I don't know, you're slightly different.'

'No, I'm not,' I persist.

'Yeah, you are,' Conor and Tom say in unison.

'Am I? In what way?'

'You are a lot more grounded,' Tom says. Conor nods.

'What? No, I'm not.' They're annoying me now.

'Yep, think you are,' Conor says adamantly. 'Think we all know why,' he continues saying. They all seem to agree.

OK, definitely time to end things soon.

Chapter Seventeen

The lads were in my head all week about me being grounded; if they noticed that, then they would expect some sort of official announcement that we were exclusive. I know I have to finish it before it goes on any longer. It won't make any sense to prolong this farce any more than I need to.

Tonight is the night. I have it all planned. A part of me does feel bad for what I am about to do. But it will be good for Tara too. Teach her a lesson; don't believe what every man tells you and especially don't think they are different from your initial theory. Most of the time, the first judgment is the true judgement.

A nice dinner, she'll think I'm such a romantic and then after I tell her, I'll pretend I feel sick and tell her I'm going to the bathroom. Not exactly polite but anyway, how else will I get out of the situation and then leave her with the bill? That is the plan, anyway.

I rang her earlier in the week and told her I wanted to take her out to dinner, no exceptions. She agreed to it straight away; normally, she has to check her roster and make sure orders are in place. I found it weird she agreed instantly and seemed excited about the dinner.

I have just showered and am putting on my shirt, I don't know why but my hands are shaking as I'm closing my buttons. I'm asking myself the questions: Why am I nervous? Will she be hurt or upset? Should I ring her and cancel tonight and just end it over the phone?

It's too late now to cancel. I am just going to go to dinner now and see how I feel as the dinner progresses. I spray on my favourite cologne and head out the door. I offered to collect her, but she said she had accounts to finish so she would meet me there instead.

I get to the restaurant, and it seems I have arrived first. The waitress shows me to our table, and I ask for a glass of whiskey. Poor woman thinks I'm about to propose; if she knew the truth, she would probably throw the whiskey at me. I take a few sips of it and then see Tara walk in. She sees me and walks towards our table. I stand and greet her with a kiss on the cheek. I take off her coat and place it behind her chair.

'Wow, this place looks lovely, Ciaran.' Tara looks around smiling and then she directs her smile at me.

'Yeah, I think it's open a few months; a few people at work came here and they said the food is nice. Do you want a drink?'

'No, I'm all right for now. Maybe later.' She takes the menu and looks at it. 'I think I'll just order something light because I had a big lunch and I'm still full.'

'Yeah, whatever you think, I might get the steak.' I look at her and she beams at me. I'm starting to feel queasy.

We order our meals and a waiter brings over a glass of wine each to our table. We look at him and then each other, puzzled. He obviously sees it in our faces because he says, 'It's complimentary tonight, we have a new wine list.'

'Oh, OK, cool, we won't complain.' I smile at Tara.

'No, definitely not, thanks.'

We look at each other and clink our glasses. 'Cheers.'

'So, how's work?'

'Oh good, very busy.'

'Did you get all the accounts done?'

'*Hmm?* Oh yeah, just a bit more, then I'm done.'

The waiter comes over and smiles and places our plates on the table. I ordered the steak and Tara ordered the fish. We talk about my work and about the stag. It feels like it's mostly me doing all the talking and Tara just barely listening. She is smiling and nodding at all the right moments, but the atmosphere feels weird. Maybe there are things going on in her life she doesn't want to talk about. But this date definitely feels cold and forced. The waiter then comes back and takes our plates.

He asks, 'How was the food?' He looks at me and Tara as he says it.

'Oh, it was lovely, thanks,' Tara says.

'Yeah, very nice, thank you,' I agree.

'Would you like a top-up of the wine?'

'No, thanks, I'm fine. It's lovely, but I'm fine,' Tara answers.

'Yeah, I'm good too,' I say.

'OK, I'll be back with the desserts.'

Tara looks around the restaurant and then at me and smiles. Maybe I should ask if she's all right. I take a sip of my water and am just about to ask how she is when ringing comes from Tara's phone. She takes it out, looks at it with puzzlement then looks at me and says, 'Oh sorry, Ciaran, I have to take this. Hello? Sorry, can't hear you, I'll have to go outside.' She holds the phone away from her ear and says, 'Sorry, Ciaran, I'll just go outside and talk, I won't be long.' She turns her head. 'Oh, it looks cold out, I'll just put on my coat, won't be long.'

'Yeah, no problem, Tara, take your time.'

She heads towards the door with the phone in her ear.

OK, so it didn't go to plan tonight. There's always the next night. I'll do it at my place, so there'll be no witnesses and be more direct and faster. No distractions.

I'm finishing off my dessert and Tara still isn't back yet. It's been ten minutes. Where is she? A waitress comes over to the table and I smile at her, but she doesn't smile at me. She just drops the bill and walks away. Very strange, and why is she giving me the bill? Are they that stuck for tables that they need us gone as soon as dessert is over?

I open the bill.

Thanks for dinner. By the way, we are over. I wouldn't bother calling me for an explanation and I am sure you know why. Your games are finished on me. BYE.

I look at the bill and the total is 165 euros. *What?* The meals were not that dear. I look down and see a bottle of wine costing 70 euros. Another bit of vengeance for Tara really rubbing salt in the wound.

I didn't see this coming. Was the waitress in on this? Or did Tara tell her before she did a runner?

I am so confused and frustrated. How could she do this?

I can't believe it. *Argh!* I'm so confused.

OK, first things first, I am going to have to pay this fecking bill. I signal a waiter and give him my card. He smiles at me, so that's good. He brings me back my card, but his smile is gone. Something clearly happened in those two minutes. *OK, I need to get out of here.*

So, I get my jacket and walk out of the restaurant. The hail that's coming down now is like rocks breaking every part of my body and self-esteem.

Hadn't planned on drinking because I wanted to be sober and not be waiting for a taxi when I dumped her, but that changed after the whiskey and wine. So, I get into the taxi in a bit of a daze. Well, I can't exactly confront her because she found out my plan and got there first. Wonder when did she find out? Did she like me? Or was she playing me from the start? I need to get home quickly.

I open the door and Tom is sitting in the kitchen.

'Hey, you are back. I thought you would be at Tara's.'

I take a beer out of the fridge. 'Yeah, no, not tonight, we kinda ended things. It was amicable. She kinda hinted and I was more than willing to follow suit, so yeah, it's finished. I'm going to go to bed, I don't really want this beer. Here, you have it.' I hand the beer to Tom and head to bed.

I didn't look at Tom's expression, just left the beer and went to my room. I hope he won't come in and check on me. I don't need any comforting words, I'm not a teenage girl, just want to be left alone. Anyway, he wouldn't be too pleased if he knew what I was planning.

I'm lying in bed, but there is no way I'll be able to sleep tonight. What the heck happened? Did I leave something like a piece of paper, and she found it? Or did I talk in my sleep? How did she know?

Was I really going to go through with my plan tonight? Did I want to do it? Was I looking for an excuse not to do it? Did she like me? Did I like her? *ARGH!*

Chapter Eighteen

It's been two months since that dreaded night. I didn't ring Tara or call her café; although, I was tempted to call in when I knew she'd be on her own in the evening and I could have it out with her, but I decided against it. She would probably relish in putting me in a situation where I turn up looking for a proper explanation and enquiring how she knew about my plan. OK, so I was going to break up with her, well... er... probably would have eventually.

I'm on the couch drinking a beer and watching a match when Tom walks in just back from work.

'Hey man, how was work?' I ask while looking at the match.

'Yeah, it was fine,' he answers. 'I was just chatting to Megan, and we might go to dinner after she visits someone. Do you want to come?' he asks.

'No, I'm OK, thanks,' I answer.

He opens the fridge and takes food out. 'So, this someone? Did she not give you a name?' I shout over to him.

'Yeah, she did, but you won't like it.'

'Oh right, that one.' *Bitch!*

'Yeah, she bought her a few groceries and comfy clothes.'

'*Hmph*, didn't think the soulless would need to eat and they have enough heat from their vile mouths to keep warm.' Stupid dig, I know, but I had to get something in.

After a few days, I had admitted Tara broke up with me and I was blindsided by it, but then I defended myself, saying it probably wasn't going to go anywhere so she saved us the hassle of me doing it further down the line. Tom agreed with me, but I could see the doubt in his eyes. But because he's a good friend, he supported my defence mechanism.

'Yeah, I know ye didn't end well, but it's still sad what she is going through. Has to be tough.'

'What is she going through?' I ask, angered that he feels sorry for Tara.

'You know about her illness.'

'What?'

'Yeah, I thought you would have heard. She got something in her lungs and it's bad, like she is really sick.'

Good enough for her, I say in my head. Don't want to say that out loud even though I am pleased she got her comeuppance. *Bitch.*

'So, what's wrong with her did you say?'

'*Ah*, I don't know the name, but it's affecting her breathing and there's not much they can do for her. It's incurable so…'

'So… what?'

'Well, like she won't last the year, they think.'

Wow, I don't like her, but I wouldn't wish that on her.
'Wow, have you seen her?'

'No, I haven't. Megan has obviously, but I can't see her, it would be too awkward. She doesn't want to see many people.'

'Yeah, right. Is she home or where is she?'

'Ah, she's home now, yeah, I think she has to have oxygen with her.'

Wow. I'm shocked.

I'm at my desk and I can't concentrate. My eyes feel so tired. I couldn't sleep at all last night thinking about what Tom told me about Tara. I really don't like her but still wouldn't want her to die. She was fine when I was 'seeing' her. How could this happen so quickly? If she were an ex, maybe I would go and see her. But she wasn't or isn't. We both played each other, and she got to break it off before I could. She got to feel the pleasure whereas I didn't, and I hated her for taking that away from me.

There's a difference here; I mean, death is so final. To never see a person again even if I despise her, she is still going to die. Why would I go and visit her? She doesn't like me, and I certainly don't like her. She'd probably throw her oxygen canister at me if she saw me. Hitting my head with the canister would give her pleasure regardless of the effects of her breathing without it.

Maybe I need to see her for myself to get some closure from everything. Although I'm a brave man to think she will want to see me. If she wasn't sick, I would never want to interact with her again, but she is, and her time is now limited. When she's gone, I know I will never see her again as opposed to maybe if her life was longer.

Death is so final. I've never had to deal with it on a close personal level before. Not that we were close; we were both playing each other, but I interacted with her often. Although it was an act on both our parts, we still saw each other a lot. Well, I'm not really sure if she was playing me or if she found out the night before she broke up with me. I do want to know what exactly happened and when and how she found out. So, I think I will have to face her, but I'll have to wear a helmet or a cup or maybe both.

I'm not even sure she'll be at her house because she's so close to her family that they would probably want her at her home house, or they'll want to stay with Tara.

I knock on her door, not expecting an answer. But then the door opens, and Mike is at the door. Oh no, I'm half expecting a punch in the face. I think I step back unknowingly to myself because Mike looks down at my feet and then up at me again, confused.

'Hey, Ciaran, good to see you, mate.' What? Is this sarcasm or is he luring me in so he can have the comfort of punching me a few times with no witnesses except Tara? But she'd obviously lie.

I don't know what to say.

'*Ah*, do you want to come inside?' He follows.

I shake my head a little to bring me back to the present. 'Sorry, I… I wasn't expecting to see you and I'm kind of expecting a punch.'

'Why? Tara broke up with you. It's very decent of you to want to visit her.'

OK, so she didn't tell him the real truth, only the part where she broke up with me. Why didn't she tell him? Maybe embarrassed that she was fooled or hurt? But no, she couldn't be hurt and even if she was, she had the upper hand. That had to cancel the hurt out.

Mike widens the door to allow me to enter. I follow him into the sitting room. Oh, the memories of being here in this very room. Tara has her back to us as we enter. Her chair is now placed in front of the TV.

'Hey, Tara, a visitor for you,' Mike says as we both stand in front of her.

'Hi, Tara,' I say.

She looks very tired, and I think my presence just made her annoyed. Well, obviously it would.

Tara is about to say something when Mike interjects 'Look,

Tara, he is here to see you. I think that trumps any bitterness between ye, he came even after you broke up with him. It's big of him to be here so just play nice and I'll go and make tea.' He smiles at Tara and then looks at me warmly and asks, 'Tea or coffee, Ciaran?'

'Coffee. Thanks, Mike.'

'Great, I'll be back in a few minutes.'

I stay standing. 'So, you didn't tell him the true story. Why?'

She stares at me. 'What does it matter to you? Oh, I see you wanted me to gloat to everyone about your pathetic plan and were expecting me to bruise your ego. Well, that's not my style.'

'No, I didn't mean…'

'Save it, Ciaran, I didn't tell him because he would have killed you and I wouldn't like to see him or anyone else go to jail for the likes of you. So, can you come up with an excuse and leave, please?' She looks back at the TV.

I'm about to go into the kitchen to Mike, but I decide I'm not going to take orders from her. I turn back and sit down. 'No, Tara, I'm not going anywhere, and you are not fit enough to leave so you are going to have to put up with my company until I decide to go…' She stares at me again. 'Look, I'm sorry, I didn't mean to insult your appearance, I just—'

Tara interjects with a burst of laughter. I'm confused; did I make a joke or is she going to tell Mike and is enjoying the future sight of me getting punched?

She finally says, 'That's the first time someone has actually insulted me since I got my diagnosis, it's quite refreshing to be treated normal and talk to me like I'm not going to break.'

'*Ahhh*... good, I guess.'

'Yeah, it's just a shame it had to come from you to feel normal.'

Mike comes in with the cups. 'I heard laughter so Ciaran must have done something right or horribly wrong and it's funny.'

We both take the cups from him and Tara answers, 'Yeah, *ahh*, you had to be here…'

'Right, well, I was planning on going to the shop for a few things so since you two haven't killed each other yet, I'm assuming it's safe for me to leave the two of ye alone for an hour.'

'Yeah, we are fine, thanks, Mike,' I say before Tara can interject.

Mike clasps his hands together. 'Right, great. Well, I'll be back in an hour so, any other thing you want, Tara?'

Tara takes a sip of her tea and answers, 'No, I'm fine, thanks.'

Mike walks out and comes back in putting his coat on, takes the keys from the table and says, 'See ye soon.'

We both say, 'Bye.'

I really don't know what way this is going to go. Is she going to bring up the elephant in the room or move on from it or just say nothing and I will have to think of topics of conversation for this next hour or so to fly by?

'Sooo…'

She starts talking before I can start it off. 'Yeah, suppose we should talk about what happened. At any other point, I wouldn't bother telling you, but seeing as though I don't have much time left, well, it has changed things. Well, I didn't expect to see you again whether I live till I'm 100 or 100 days.'

'Look maybe, Tara, we should just leave it.'

'No, because you are the type that would want to know, and I would like to brag how I got the upper hand and not you.'

I really want to leave, but how can I be rude to a sick person?

I'll go straight down if I do, and I need all the brownie points I can get.

'So, when did you find out?'

'Who says I didn't know all along?'

'What?'

'I was suspicious after the hen party; you were way too nice. My opinion of you never bothered you so why be nice to me suddenly? At the wedding, I did think I was wrong about you. You were respectful to everyone and sweet to people. Then when you saw me and Paul in the bar, you didn't look jealous, you looked annoyed like he was messing up something.'

'You got that from one look?'

'Yeah, I own a café, I deal with customers regularly. I learn to read whether people have a bad day or got dumped or lost their job or are happy with themselves.'

'So, why continue?'

'Because I was still doubting myself about you. Then the night we went away and you set your alarm, I used your face to turn it off and scrolled down by mistake and saw in your reminder: "break up night". I was fit to kill you, but then I thought again, what would it feel like for him to feel the effect of his plan on himself? I did plan on a big spectacle of getting everyone together and blowing up your reminder for everyone to see, but then I thought there would be some eejit there who would feel sorry for you. It started with our mutual dislike towards one another; it can finish with hatred between the two of us. That's why I didn't tell people the truth. It's between us and nobody has to feel awkward or take sides. I know you planned a big spectacle and wanted to brag how you fooled me, so I am proud I was able to prevent that, but I am not proud of what happened mostly because I am annoyed that I didn't listen to my gut and believe you were full of crap.'

'Look when it came to that night to break up with you, I found I was hesitant, and I didn't know why, but what really angered me was that you didn't seem hesitant at all. You just did it and walked out. But I suppose I get it now, you dumped the egotistic, arrogant and selfish Ciaran. So, I can't blame you for doing that. But you should know, not that it matters, but I did have doubts and if I'm being honest, I don't think I would have ended things and hoped you would never know what I had initially planned.'

There is silence in the room for what feels like hours until Tara finally speaks again.

'I don't regret that I ended it, I just wish...' She throws her hands in the air. '*Argh!* I don't know what I wish.'

'Yeah, I don't know either.' I sip my coffee, but it's gone cold, I'm assuming hers is too. 'I may not be the best cook, but I can boil a kettle, do you want another cup of tea?'

Tara looks at her cup. '*Ah*, yeah, OK, thanks.'

I take her cup and go into the kitchen. Think we both needed a breather. I rinse the cups and put a teabag into each cup and look out the window while I wait for the kettle to boil. I hear sniffling coming from Tara, she can't be crying. If she is, then it must have to do with her illness. I should leave her alone in case she doesn't want me to hear, but if it continues, I'll go in. The kettle is boiled so I pour the water into them and get the milk from the fridge, she doesn't take sugar and I'm not going to have some either. I make noise loud enough to give her time to compose herself. I walk back in.

'Now, hope the tea is nice. I thought it would be nicer without the drop of poison, so enjoy.'

I smile at her, and she laughs back at me and clicks her

fingers. 'Damn, you saw where I keep the poison, I'll have to change that later.'

We talk about everything and anything, there are laughs and some tears until Mike returns. I stay for another half hour and help clear up. I get my jacket and Mike walks me out.

'Thanks for coming, Ciaran,' Mike says as I'm putting on my jacket. 'Her mood has picked up today and it's because you came.' He leans in close. 'She won't admit that though, so will you call again?'

'*Ah*, well, I don't know if it was me. Maybe I was just lucky with her mood. I will call but if Tara doesn't want me to call, then I won't,' I whisper to Mike.

Mike winks at me. 'Do call again.'

I pat down my jacket for my keys, and I realise I left them in the sitting room. 'OK, Mike, *ah*, I left my keys, so I'll just go and get them.'

I go into the sitting room and Tara is on her phone looking through pictures. I notice the one of me and her, but I look away as soon as she looks back at me. 'Sorry, I forgot my keys.'

'Oh, right, I thought they were Mike's. Sorry, I would have called you back if I knew.'

'Oh, no worries.' I toss my keys a few times in the air. '*Ahhm*, Mike asked me to call again.' I tilt my head towards the door where Mike is. 'What do you think? I mean, if you want to just leave it at this nice, pleasant moment and let it be a nice memory or I could call again and risk the throwing of knives and daggers? Up to you.'

Tara looks at the TV. '*Ah*...' She turns to me. 'Maybe we could risk another encounter, as a test on whether we can hold on to our weapons.'

I look down at my keys and fiddle with them. 'OK, cool, I'll message you when I am free again. I didn't mean 'cos I'm so busy and I'll call whenever I get time, *ah*... I just meant when I'm finished work or if you are free... *ahh*, this isn't coming out right, sorry.'

Tara bats her hand away. 'Ciaran, it's fine. I know what you mean.'

I skim my foot towards the door. 'OK, I'm gonna leave before I say anything that will put my foot in it. Bye.'

I open the door and Mike is on the phone at the back door. He holds the phone away from his ear, smiles and says, 'Bye, Ciaran, see you again.'

'Yeah, thanks for the coffee, Mike.'

Mike continues talking on the phone, and I leave. I am in such a trance, I have no idea where I will go next because I don't feel like heading home yet. It was definitely not what I was expecting, I thought I would have a bruise on my cheek or a sore back from being shoved against a wall. How could I blame her for being mad at me? And yet, after her harsh vent, she was pleasant, considerate, mannerly and kind. I am the worst person in the world for wanting to treat her so badly. I put my head in my hands and then start the ignition and head home, I'm too tired to even go to the pub to drown my sorrows and alleviate my horrible behaviour.

Chapter Nineteen

I knock on the door; I hear movement on the other side. I hope I didn't wake her. The door opens. She looks tired, but I think it's best I act like I don't notice. I part my lips wide, smiling.

'Hey, I brought some food to make dinner, hope you are hungry.' I hold up the bags waiting for her to open the door wide.

'Oh, thanks, Ciaran, but—'

I hold my hand up. '*Ahhh*, look, if you don't want it, you don't have to eat it and if you don't feel like company, well... I'll stay in the kitchen. I have tests to mark anyway, and Tom and Megan are at my place, so you'd be doing me a favour. Please?' I beam my killer smile at her.

She rolls her eyes. 'OK, fine, come in. But you are warned, I will not be good company. So, if I come across rude, well, it's because I mean to be.' She smiles.

'That's fine, I'm used to it by now.' I smile back as I walk towards the kitchen.

I empty the contents on the counter and look in the press for the pots and chopping board.

'Thanks for doing this.'

I turn and see Tara standing with her oxygen in her nose. She obviously took it off to answer the door. 'Yeah, no problem. Like I said, you are doing me the favour. *Ah*, so how are you feeling?' I ask as I put the chopping board on the counter.

'Yeah, OK, feel a bit tired today.'

'Yeah, hey, sit down and I'll make you tea or hot chocolate

or whatever you want.' Tara looks at me. 'Sorry, I'm not trying to make you feel like an invalid, I just—'

'No, sorry, Ciaran, I just got a twinge in my back and I'm trying to deal with the pain. It's eased a bit now, yeah, so tea would be nice. Thanks.'

'Great.' I turn to put water into the kettle.

'So, what are you cooking?'

'*Ah,* lasagne, I thought it would be a nice change and put my cooking skills to the test, but if it's not nice, I have a number in my phone that I'll use and play it off as my own.' I laugh.

'That sounds nice, I'll ignore the doorbell when it rings.'

'Yeah, if you could.'

'Sure, I'll leave you to it.' She turns for the sitting room.

I bring in the tea to Tara and she's reading. She puts down the book and smiles as I leave the tea on the table. 'Thanks, Ciaran.'

'No problem. I put my hands on my hips. 'So, is it a good book?'

She takes the tea from the table. '*Hmm?* Oh yeah, it is good, she's married a man and has found a secret about him, so it's about who is he really? And what's he hiding. So, it's good so far, kind of addictive.'

'Great, I'll let you get back to it.'

'*Ah.* Well... I was gonna take a break so if you want to get a cup and sit down.'

'Yeah, OK, I'll be right back.'

I put a spoon of coffee into a cup, pour water into it and sit down in the chair opposite Tara. She smiles at me when I sit, and I can tell she's waiting to say something.

'So, how's work?'

I sip my coffee and say, 'Yeah, it's fine. Same old thing

every day, one of the teachers is on maternity leave so a new one started Monday and she's nice, and very optimistic, but give her time and that will all go.'

'*Haaa*, yeah, like us all, but I did love my café, so I will miss that.'

I look at her, waiting for her to tell me more. I must have a confused face on me because she continues, 'Oh yeah, I had to sell it to some big corporation because no one was going to take it over and I couldn't wait around for someone to buy it, so I just got Mike to ask around and explain the situation and one of his friends got in contact with another business and they contacted me soo... I don't know if the place will be sold again or if something else will open or maybe they'll keep it open, but I couldn't deal with the headache, so I just needed it sorted quickly. I'm sure the staff are annoyed and disappointed, but that's life.'

'Oh, wow, Tara, I'm sorry about that.'

'Yeah, me too.'

As if on cue, the timer buzzes on the oven. 'I'll just finish in the kitchen and put it in the oven and then I'll be back, Tara.'

'Yeah, work away, thanks.'

I finish preparing the ingredients, put them in the oven and rejoin Tara in the sitting room. She tells me about her diagnosis, how she noticed something different and how it felt to be told the life-changing news. At times, she got teary but moved past it. I wasn't sure if I should've comforted her, so I remained seated. She confessed that she was scared of what lay ahead when the time came and hoped it wouldn't be a long-drawn-out process. It was when she said that that I got up instinctively from my seat and comforted her. She tried to hold back crying.

'I'm sorry, I don't know why I'm crying, like I've known

what was ahead for a while.' She grabs a tissue and wipes her eyes.

'It's fine, Tara, there's a difference between hearing it and then telling it to someone; especially the first time because I didn't want to ask, I just knew it wasn't good news you got.'

'Yeah.' She takes a deep breath. 'I think that's it and the fact that I feel a bit more fatigued than first being diagnosed, you know I had more energy whereas now... just... yeah, not as much.'

'Yeah, I mean obviously I have no idea what you are going through, but all I can do is agree that it's a shit situation you are dealing with and cook you lasagne.'

She smiles at that, then as if on cue the oven timer dings. 'Right on time,' Tara says.

'Yeah, weird, I'll just prepare, so come out in five minutes,' I say. I tap her on the knee and go to the kitchen.

Wow, that was a lot of information to process, it's crazy how someone's life can change so quickly. One minute, Tara was healthy with her own business; next, her business is gone, and her time is limited and there's nothing that can be done about it either. Fighting won't change the prognosis, all that one has is acceptance for the shit outcome. How can life be so cruel? She didn't deserve this.

I quickly run to the bathroom to wipe my eyes and come out trying to keep a smile on my face and the mood upbeat. I have no right to cry, it's not me going through this. All I can do is keep her smiling and take her mind off this awful situation for as long as possible.

Tara joins me in the kitchen. 'Hey, here, take a seat.' I take the chair out for her; she sits and pushes it in. 'Wow, this looks lovely, Ciaran. Thanks.'

'No problem. Hopefully, it is nice. I followed the recipe anyway, so I'll blame the chef I looked up if it tastes bad.'

'No, no, I'm sure it's lovely.'

'Great. Well, tuck in.' She takes a bit of the lasagne and blows on it and then puts it into her mouth. I hold off until she tastes it first.

I watch with tenterhooks as she puts it into her mouth, she makes a face. 'Is it good or bad?' I ask.

She nods as she chews. '*Hmmm*, lovely sorry… just hot, but yeah, very nice. You'll see for yourself or taste for yourself, *haha*.'

I laugh and take a bite. 'Yeah, it is nice, seems the chef knew what he was doing,' I joke.

We eat in silence; I am shocked at how good the meal is and I'm sure Tara is too, but she won't admit it. She's nodding a lot as she eats and she's opening and closing her eyes as she eats. I would take that as a good sign. We both clear our plates and I wash up. Tara informed me she had a dishwasher that I could use, but it was two plates and glasses; it would be quicker and more economical to wash them in the sink. I sit back down at the table and Tara shows me a photo of herself and Mike. They have muck all over their clothes and are laughing. I never noticed it behind the table.

'*Awh*, that's a nice photo, how old were ye?' I ask.

'*Ah*, Mike was twelve and I was ten, it was such a random day. We weren't supposed to be going to our aunt's but my father fell at work so he went to the hospital. So, Mum went to him but didn't want us in the hospital, so she dropped us at our aunt's. She was feeding lambs and brought us out, there's was water to one side where the hose was, it was boiling out so, of course, we went over and Mike turned on the hose. He surprised me and sprayed me with it and I fell back, landed on the ground where it was wet. He felt bad and told me to do it to him, so I did, and we then just sat in the muck splashing each other. My aunt then turned around thinking we were watching her, but nope. She ran over to us. "Oh my god, ye scamps, what are ye doing?" She was so mortified and agitated, then she just looked at us and laughed. She ran in and got her camera and took the photo, then ordered us out and forced us into the shower and got clean clothes. "Oh, if your mother saw this, she'd be saying, one job you had. We'll tell her eventually but not today, OK, I'll give her the photo," she said. It was so random how muck made us laugh so much, but I think my aunt was glad we were having fun because she didn't know if it was bad with my father. But thankfully, he was fine, he was dehydrated and out again later that day.'

'That is a nice memory.'

'Yeah, must give this photo to Mike.' She looks at it warmly. 'Now, we'll have something to finish off the meal nicely, we'll have a small nightcap.'

'Tara, I can get it.'

'Nonsense, I can walk to the press. The meal was lovely, must get the recipe off you and try to achieve it myself.'

'Yeah, sure, I'll write it down.'

As Tara goes to the press, I get a pen and paper and write down the recipe and method. She pours a splash of whiskey into two glasses and brings them over to the table, then stalls.

'Actually, we'll go into the sitting room and have them, be more comfortable.' She smiles, and I follow her to the sitting room. She puts them on the coffee table and sits on the couch. I take my glass and sit on the chair. She takes a sip and makes a squeamish face.

'Is this your first time to have whiskey?'

'No, I've had it a few times, but I hate it.'

I look at her and she knows what I'm about to say next.

'I know, then why am I drinking it? There were a few nights where I wasn't getting any sleep and I was so dizzy and fatigued, so my mum suggested to try a bit of whiskey... hot whiskey. She was like just humour me please. If it doesn't work, then no harm done. So, she made me one. I took little sips and had a great sleep after taking it, it like calmed my whole body and I was able to just close my eyes and sleep. Now I'm not trying to advertise it as a great cure and like the best drink ever. But it did work for me and given my circumstances, I'm not too worried about moderation and alcohol being bad for your health. It helps me sleep and that's the main thing and it's a few sips so...' She takes another sip and squirms again.

'Oh yeah, anything that helps. I know after a stag party I was at last year, it was a weekend one and I got feck all sleep. When I went home, I couldn't talk to anyone because I was so irritable. Everything annoyed me; the radio and doors banging and that was from not getting sleep. It really improves people's mood when they get it. Even a shit situation can look better the next day.' I close my eyes after I say it. Feck! I open them again. 'Sorry, Tara, a new day won't help what you are going through.'

'It's fine, Ciaran, I knew what you meant.'

We chat for another hour and I can see she is getting tired. It's time to leave.

I get up. 'OK, Tara, not to be rude but you look tired, so I don't want to exhaust you. I'll call back again, all right?'

'Yeah, OK. Thanks, Ciaran.'

'When will Mike be back? Or is someone else coming?'

'Ah, Mike is gone away for the night with Rachel. My mother is coming tomorrow.'

'Oh, so are you on your own tonight?'

'Yeah, but I don't mind, it's nice for a change.'

I mess with my keys in my pocket. I can't leave her.

'*Ah*, not to sound rude or forward, but I can stay tonight. I'm not busy with anything. If you want, I won't take offence if you tell me to leave.'

She purses her lips and looks around the room. I really don't know what she will say.

'Yeah, OK, that's fine. If you don't mind now?'

'No, not at all,' I clasp my hands. 'Great, so, I'll get another splash of whiskey from the kitchen since we aren't driving tonight.'

I bring back the two glasses and we sit and watch a TV show that Tara likes. When it's over, Tara gets up but she seems fragile. I don't want her to feel like I'm her saviour by offering a hand, but I don't want to see her struggling either so at the risk of getting my head cut off, I say, 'Hey, Tara, do you want help?'

'Yeah, I would. Sorry, I just need a link up 'cos my legs get a bit stiff.'

'Yeah, no problem.' I take her hand and slowly walk with her to her room. I pull back the covers and she sits on the side of the bed and then lies back slowly.

'Are you OK now? Do you want me to bring you water?'

'No, I have a bottle on the floor there.' She points to the ground, so I pick it up and put it on her locker.

'Do you need anything else?' I ask.

'No, I'm fine, thanks.' She pulls the covers up and looks at me with tired eyes.

'All right, Tara, I'll let you sleep, but ring if you want anything.'

'Thanks, Ciaran.' I turn off the light and leave.

I get up early and look in the fridge for food. She has stuff for a fry, so I decide to put it on.

As I'm frying the last of the rashers, I hear, 'Hey, Ciaran, you don't have to cook, I'll do that.'

I turn around to Tara and say, 'No, you won't. Sit down, and it'll be all ready in five minutes.'

'Well, I'll just make tea if that's all right. I won't interfere with your lovely meal.'

'All right. I'll allow,' and I move to one side to let her boil the kettle.

'So did you have a good sleep?' I ask.

'I did, think I was gone soon after I hit the pillow. I had such a nice dream; I was in New York and I was going to see the Statue of Liberty then I was in Central Park talking to Bon Jovi. It was weird but made sense at the time. It's weird that dreams can connect with your thoughts.'

'Oh really, were you thinking about New York like when you were there last?'

'No, I was never there. Always wanted to go, but now I never will. It would have been definitely on my bucket list. Were you ever there?'

'Yeah, years ago, I did a J1, but I think we only saw like three sightseeing parts. I'd like to go again to see all the other parts of Manhattan and the other boroughs.'

'Yeah, that would be nice. Anyway, can I get a plate? Smells lovely.'

'Yeah, get a plate and I'll put them on for you.'

As we are eating, Helen knocks and opens the door. '*Yohoo*, anyone home?' she shouts as she walks in.

'*Awh*, hello, Ciaran, how are you?'

I stand to hug her. 'Yeah, I'm good, thanks. Do you want some of a fry? There's plenty left on the hob there.' I point over towards the cooled-down hob. Hopefully, it's still warm for Helen.

'Yeah, sure, I may as well, thanks.' She gets a plate from the press and uses her hands to throw some of the fry on her plate and then gets a knife and fork from the drawer.

'So, Ciaran, anything strange or exciting in your neck of the woods?'

'His neck of the woods is about ten minutes from here so, Mum, if there was something exciting, we would all hear,' Tara interjects for me. I smile at her assertiveness.

'*HOO*, looks like someone got to sleep last night. Very quick and alert today,' Helen responds scornfully. Tara rolls her eyes.

'So, where's Dad?' Tara asks.

'Oh, he's gone off with your uncle to help him choose a tractor, waste of time. It's impossible for that man to make a decision. He's always humming and hawing with things before he decides. He'll want him to go somewhere else next week to look at another one.'

'Yeah, my Uncle Marty, takes his time, he can be tight too. He might buy something cheap, but it'll break and then he'll pay to get it fixed whereas if he spent a bit more, it would last and it would actually save him money. But you can't tell him,' Tara says to me.

'Maybe it's men, Ciaran; they can be extremely cautious or extremely impulsive.'

'Yes, Mum, I know what you mean,' Tara says with a harsh attitude. She turns to me again. 'Dad bought a car last year without telling Mum, and she wasn't very happy. Were you!' she says.

'No, I wasn't, like how he could go off and spend money without even mentioning a car? It had me worried he was going through a mid-life crisis. I was fretting for a month waiting to see if he'd land home with a twenty-two-year-old blonde and want me out.'

Tara and I both snigger and Tara assists with the topic of conversation. 'Thankfully, he didn't; it was impulsive, but he always wanted a car like the one he has and it was on sale or whatever the word is. It had come down in price anyway so he bought it and no problems with it, which was good because normally there can be. When you buy something at a lower price, it can end up costing more.'

'Yeah, he didn't trade me in anyway. Well, maybe he did for the car because he loves that car, but I'll take it over another woman any day.'

'Yeah, good for him,' I say. Probably a weird reply, but I felt I needed to say something to recognise I was listening to the two of them.

Chapter Twenty

I get back to the house and Conor is in the kitchen making coffee.

'Hey, where were you? Out with a woman?' he asks cheekily.

'No, I stayed at Tara's. She didn't look great last night so I thought it would be safer to stay.'

'*Awh*, that's nice. It's very big of you to help her after what she did to you.'

'Well, it wasn't entirely her fault.'

'Oh, are you gushing over her again?'

'No, just that I was bitter at first, so I put all the blame on her, but the truth is, I was planning on breaking up with her and she saw it on my phone and got there first.'

'What? Why? Was it because we said you changed with her? Did we freak you out?'

'No, it wasn't that. I suppose I knew her and I kinda wanted to mess with her head, because I knew she didn't like me. It started off as a game and then, I don't know, when ye said I changed, then yeah, I just wanted to finish the "game" quick because the longer it went on, the more I would just keep procrastinating and would always be in the back of mind. Even if I started to like her and we got, I don't know, serious, it would always feel like it's hanging over me. I had to end it, but then she saw it on my phone and got there before me. Obviously, she was mad over what I was going to do.'

'Right, so does she forgive you now or?'

'No, not really. Suppose maybe, I don't know. She's tolerating me anyway. Maybe she's too tired to be angry with me. I don't know. I know it was an ass move but—'

'Yeah, it was an ass move, especially when she was sick.'

'Hey, she didn't get sick till after she broke up with me. I'm a prick, but I'm not that bad. I have some morals, not a lot but some.'

'*Hmm*, right. So, how is she overall?'

'Suppose she has good days and bad, but, overall, it's probably hard to accept the rapid change in her life and knowing what is to come. I suppose it's not the illness giving her bad days, more so the horrible situation when she thinks about it.'

'Yeah, like I can't understand how she's feeling, but I can empathise that it's a shit situation.'

'Yeah, it is.'

'Did Tom know about your plan?'

'No, I didn't tell anyone, but I did tell him after.'

'*Ohhh*, not happy, I'd say. He's a sensitive soul, our Tom.'

'Yeah, he was a bit annoyed and then he was like, "Yeah, I was wondering why you were so adamant to *date* her", – he used air quotes for date – 'then he said, "Well, you got your comeuppance. Good for Tara." So he was glad it worked out for her and not for me. Couldn't really argue with him.'

'Yeah, fair enough. So, is she on her own now?'

'No, her mother came so I left them alone. Think I'm just going to go to bed because I slept on the couch and although it was comfy, I was conscious Tara might need me, so I didn't want to fall into a deep sleep.'

'Yeah, OK, I'll chat to you in a bit.'

I head down into my room, put my phone on silent, lie down on the bed and close my eyes.

I wake up and see that I got a message from Tara, thanking me for staying last night and for breakfast. I send back an emoji with a smile and red cheeks. I didn't do much, just put on a few sausages, rashers and eggs for us both; it was mostly for my benefit because I was starved.

I go outside for a walk and cannot stop thinking about what Tara said regarding New York. She always wanted to go. I mean there's no way I could bring her because we would be conscious of her breathing, she wouldn't enjoy it. It wouldn't be fair to force it on her and knowing herself, she wouldn't be able to go. It would be cruel. But maybe there's a way I could bring some snippet of New York to her. Get some personal photos, not the landscape ones on Google or selfies of the places, that would be weird. I could look through my iCloud for my photos and ask my friends for photos they took of New York minus themselves in them. I could ask around for videos of horse and carriage in Central Park and horns blaring to really make her feel she's in New York. Nothing says New York like blaring car horns. It may take a few days; well, hopefully, it will only take a few days. But anyway, I'll ask around and get whatever I can, and it will be something anyway.

Chapter Twenty-One

Things are coming together for my New York plan for Tara. I got a load of photos from friends and others who put some scenic ones up on social media platforms. I had a few videos myself from New York. I saw others that the five of us recorded; oh lord, we were so lame! Obviously, I didn't choose them, felt like deleting them, but they might be nice to have in twenty years' time. I ordered a poster of Bon Jovi from when he played Madison Square Garden and put that on the flash drive so she can watch it after the photos, and I'll put up the poster because there usually are plenty of them before entering the concert. Then I got a few friends to wish her a happy trip to New York at the start of the creation. I hope she likes it. I actually got really into it, so if she doesn't like it, well, I wouldn't mind watching it anyway.

I rang Mike and told him my plan and wondered if he and the family wanted to join the New York night, but he said he would leave it to the two of us. So, I am going to hers tonight to unveil the memento. I don't know why they wouldn't come. It's not like it's a romantic gesture. I mean, we are not dating, it's just something to give a woman who is sick a nice memory. Mike was so sly when I said it to him. It was mostly '*Oohh*' and '*Awhhh*' with everything I mentioned. Maybe I shouldn't have done this; it's amazing how you could have a nice idea and people then perceive it as something else and then there's pressure and constant awareness of trying to emphasise the first idea, not the other idea with the physical aspect.

Argh! *I have it planned now, so I'm just going to do it.*

I knock on Tara's door as I open it, she's expecting me so she left it ajar, and said it would save time for her answering it.

'Hey, Tara! I'm here.'

I go into the kitchen, she's not there; I look in the sitting room, not there. I shout again and she comes out of her room. 'Sorry, Ciaran, I was just changing, I was in my pyjamas all day and it wouldn't be appropriate to still be in them.'

She fixes her top. 'That's all right, Tara, you could have stayed in them.'

'No, no, it's not good to be in them all day anyway, makes a person lazy. So, what are you cooking?'

'*Ah*, it's a surprise actually. I'm going to have to ask you to make yourself scarce for about forty-five minutes. I know it's very rude, but I think you will like it. So, if you could, please!'

'Yeah, I'll go into the sitting room.'

'*Ah* no, I need to use that too, so I'm sorry but I have to send you to your room for forty-five minutes.' She looks at me. 'Sorry, Tara,' I say again. If she doesn't like this plan, then I will be running out the door.

'*Ammm*... OK, fine. If this is some weird prank, I'm telling you now, I will be pissed and I don't want some elaborate surprise where there's like fifty people in the kitchen. So, tell them to leave if you have that arranged.'

'OK, there'll be a slight change of plan for the night, better start making calls,' I say. She stares at me. *OK, better make it clear that there won't be a party.* 'Joking, nothing like that, just a bit of food and a movie and there won't be anyone else, I swear. So, does that give you solace? Will you go to your room, please?'

She purses her lips. 'OK, I will chance it, but I will be turning if it is something more.'

'Yeah, that's fine, but you won't because it's nothing like that.'

'Right, so how long again am I banished to my room?' she asks.

'Forty-five minutes, I'll start a timer.'

'Right, see you in forty-five, so,' she says with a hint of nervousness in her tone.

'Great.' I smile as she turns towards her room and closes the door.

OK, a bit of an apprehensive start, but I'll kick on anyway. I go out to the car to bring in the bags. I start putting up the poster in the sitting room and setting up the memory stick in the TV along with hanging a few American banners. I put up another poster that contains all the famous Broadway productions and put a light I got on Amazon that has different colour lights beside it to give some effect to the poster. I downloaded music taken from the productions and put them on my phone, the songs will be playing when I bring her in here.

Next up is the food, God bless modern-day grocery shops having different cuisines of food. In the American section, I got hot dogs, bagels, chips, cookies and burgers. I put the chips and burgers in the air fryer and while they're cooking, I set up the burger buns, cookies, bagels, salad and meat and place them on the table. I am singing to "Mama Mia" as I'm setting up the food. *What has become of me?* When the chips and burgers are cooked, I place them on a plate. I give the air fryer a quick wipe then put in the hotdogs.

After I do that, I knock on Tara's door. With all the preparation and limited time, I didn't take a minute to be nervous. Now I am!

Tara comes out and says, 'So, do you need more time to

make more calls?'

'No, all done, no one is coming, all cancelled. Stuck with me,' I say with a wide smile.

She makes a disgusted face and then says, 'Oh OK, you'll do.' She smiles then and I lead her out to the kitchen first.

As she looks around and at the table, I remember the hot dogs are in the air fryer, so I run over and take them out. I leave them on a plate and then look at Tara. She is gobsmacked.

'Oh my god, what did you do?' she looks at me and shakes her head. 'Oh my god!'

'Well, I thought I'd bring a taste of New York to you. There's American bagels, hotdogs without queuing up at a vendor and cookies, chips and other bits of food. So, you want to sit and try it?'

'Yeah, of course.' She turns and looks at me curiously. 'Is that the Lion King coming from the sitting room?'

'Yeah, it is, it's all the Broadway famous productions.'

She walks in and puts her hands to her mouth. I didn't really have a chance to look at it from the kitchen and when I go over to see, it actually looks cool. I turned off the light and left on the multi-coloured lights beside the poster and my phone playing in that corner. Yeah, it does look very well, I'm impressed with it myself. She turns to face me, and she has tears in her eyes.

'This is so nice, I can't believe you did this, I really don't know what to say.'

'Well, we'll eat firs—' She grabs me and hugs me while trying to retain her tears. We stay that way for a few minutes, I think, and we both say nothing. Tara then lets go and takes a seat.

'I'm still speechless,' she says. And then follows with 'Thank you for doing this, it's just unbelievable.'

'*Aw*, no problem, now let's eat. Might have to heat up the

hot dogs and burgers.'

'No it's fine, I don't like it too hot anyway.'

'Well, there's not too hot and then there's cold, so if you want anything heated let me know.'

She takes the burger and bun and puts salad and sauce on her bun, then takes chips and a hotdog. She takes a bite of her hotdog. 'It's lovely, Ciaran, thanks.'

I do the same, I take the burger and chips and then the hotdog. I follow her lead and try the hotdog first. Yeah, it does taste nice. We eat in silence and look at each other every now and again as we eat.

When we finish, I take all the plates and put them in the dishwasher and the food not eaten I put into a bowl that Tara can either have for later or give to her mother for their dog. Tara offered to help, but I said, 'If you were in New York, you wouldn't be helping the staff clean, so let me tidy up.' She didn't protest, she decided to eat some of the cookies and sing to a song from *Wicked*. (She told me when the song started).

'Now all done, do you want to go into the sitting room?'

Her eyes widen. 'Yeah, finally.'

I roll my eyes at her and she smiles. 'OK, so take a seat and I will start the mini slide show of our sightseeing tour of New York.'

'What, I thought we were going to listen to all the songs from Broadway.'

'Well, that's for the starts but,' I say defensively.

'No, no, sorry, I meant I wasn't expecting any more.'

'Oh right, yep more to come.' I turn the TV for the memory stick option and then press play. 'OK, here we go, so where will we start first, *ah*, has to be the Empire State Building.'

The memory stick goes through all the sightseeing areas

around New York, there is a seven-second pause for every photo. Tara is mesmerised by all the places, there has been no talk between us since it started. It then comes to Tiffany's, and I pause it. 'Hey, why did you pause it?'

'Because we are going to have breakfast at Tiffany's, I'll be right back.' I get up and she watches as I leave. I boil the kettle, make two lattes and bring out two pain au chocolat that are in two brown bags. I smile at her as I give her the latte.

'Oh my God, Ciaran, I don't think I will be able to put this all into words until tomorrow, even maybe the next day. So, when I have words, I will text or ring you but know that this is magical and beautiful, thank you so much.'

'You're welcome, Tara, I'm glad you liked the whole night.' I sit and we both drink our lattes and eat our pain au chocolat. It's not until I see how much she is enjoying this and appreciating it that I can't believe I did something like this.

'So, next up now, we are going to Madison Square garden where the brilliant Bon Jovi is playing, but sorry before you think I did something elaborate or unbelievable, it's not a live concert and unfortunately, I have no contacts that could contact Jon Bon Jovi to give you a nice message. It's a concert that was on a few years ago, but I did hang up a poster to give the concert a personal feeling that you are there.'

She looks around for the poster. 'Oh my God, I didn't even see that, sorry, I was looking at the Broadway and the TV. Wow! Can't believe you bought that!'

'Well, you know when people go to Madison, there's like posters everywhere of the concert, I saw it on a film once, so I thought it would give an exciting feel before the concert starts now.'

'*Awh*, that's so nice. Can I keep the poster?'

'Yeah, it's yours, I'm hardly going to hang it and then take it back for myself.'

'Well, maybe, if you liked him, you'd like the poster back. It's like on *Friends* when Rachel thought Joey gave the baby Hugsy and Joey said no, that's just to show where the baby will go. Could be the same; just to give an exciting feeling before watching the concert.'

'OK, well, it's not, the poster is yours, now I'll just move to the concert.'

'OK, great,' Tara says as she puts on a jumper that was behind the chair. 'Now, I'm ready when you are!'

I click on PLAY and the concert starts.

'I sometimes eat popcorn before a concert. Do you want me to make some?'

'*Ah*, yeah, maybe at intermission,' Tara says, smiling.

When the concert is over, I look over at Tara and she is beaming. 'Oh my god, that was a great concert, and the seats were brilliant,' she says boldly.

'Yeah, it was really good. They're great showmen!'

'Yeah, they really are and it's great I don't have far to go home and didn't have the worry of people looking at me.' She laughs and takes a last sip of her drink.

'Does it bother you that much using the oxygen?' I ask.

'Yeah, it does, it really does. It's embarrassing, like I know no one would laugh. Well, maybe some assholes, but it's the pity look I'd rather avoid as much as I can. So, it was actually so nice seeing New York and experiencing bits of New York without having to leave my house. Really appreciate you doing this. Thank you.'

'Yeah, glad you enjoyed it, and for the record you are not defined by your oxygen tank, well, definitely not to me, anyway.'

She looks at me warmly.

'Now on that corny note, I'll tidy up here. Do you want anything?'

'No, I'm fine, thanks.'

I bring out the glasses and the bowls and put them in the sink. May as well wash them and not have Tara doing it. I go back into the sitting room and Tara's eyes are closed.

'Hey, Tara, do you want to go to bed? I can leave.'

She opens her eyes and says, 'No, I'm not tired. I was going over all the photos in my head.'

'Oh right, well, I can leave now if you want time to yourself.'

She purses her lips and clicks her tongue. '*Am*, no, you can stay for another while if it suits? If you want, you can stay in Mike's room, well, it's the spare room but Mike is here a lot so we call it his room. Save your back from lying on the couch.'

'*Am*, yeah. OK.' I slap both my knees. 'So, what do you wanna do next, this was the last of my plan. After the concert was over, I was going to just leave so now the plan has changed.'

'Well, I'm going to make more popcorn and let you decide what we are going to watch.' She gets up and goes into the kitchen.

I have no clue what to pick, I go through the As and the Bs and then see *Batman Begins*. I love this film, haven't seen it in a while. I hope Tara approves this choice. I hit PLAY as Tara walks in with the popcorn.

'So, what film?' Then she looks. '*OOOH*, Batman. I love this film.'

'Really?'

'Oh yeah, Cristian Bale and the way he says "I'm Batman", oh yeah, so cool. I haven't watched this in ages. We should do the trilogy, but not tonight because I'll just fall asleep. Sorry, not to sound presumptuous.'

'No. Yeah. Definitely, we'll watch them all another night.'

'Cool, do you want a drink with your popcorn?' Tara asks.

'*Ah*, yeah, I'll get them.'

I know I have seen a lot of her these last few weeks, but I don't know, is this dating or is it just spending time with a friend I used to pretend date? Obviously, I like spending time with her, and I think she does too, but we both know what is down the road so there's no point in putting that kind of pressure on each other. This isn't some Nicholas Sparks novel where I ask her what's number one on her list and try to achieve it all for her. Its real life and real life is complicated. Think we both know this is just friends and maybe in different circumstances, it may have been more but it's not. These are the cards dealt and the best I should do for Tara is keep her smiling till the end. Now that I have cleared that up in my head, I can now focus on the movie.

I walk in with the two drinks and say, 'Sorry, Tara, I was just texting my brother, I have to tax his car for him.'

That is true, but instead of tonight him texting me it was two days ago. 'He's gone to Portugal for two weeks and forgot to tax it.'

'Oh right, very nice.'

'Yeah, lucky for some... Sorry, Tara, I just meant it as a dig for him, not us, and he's not even here. So, I don't know why I said it. I should've just said, "yeah, it's great for him".'

'It's fine, I would say the same if it was Mike, think it's just something you say when it's family. If it were someone else, you'd say oh that's nice, but prob secretly thinking, feckers! The good thing about family is you say what you think and not really bother if they take offence.'

'Yeah, it's true, isn't it?' I say loudly because I'm glad

someone understands.

'Yep.'

We watch all the movie and then Tara heads to her room and I head to Mike's room. The bed is so comfy. I walked beside her as she went to her room; she was able to get to her room without help but as she said herself, having me beside her gave her security and confidence. She insisted I stay the night and gave me a hug before she went to her room. So here I am, feeling very pleased with myself. I mean, I knew she would like it, but then I was also anxious it may have made her feel sad that she'll never be able to go and it.

Now after seeing her so happy with the night made me feel glad that I did it for her.

I waken to the smell of sausages and rashers. *Oh crap, she made breakfast.* I can hear music and talking. The radio must be on or she's on the phone. I look at my phone and its half ten. Well, time I got up. She probably thinks I'm so lazy. I throw on my clothes and head out to the kitchen. I hear laughing and another voice. OK, so she's not on the phone. I walk in and Mike is turning the rashers and Tara is sitting at the table looking at her phone.

'Morning,' I say.

They both look up. 'Oh, morning, Ciaran,' Mike says and Tara smiles. 'Did you have a nice sleep?'

'Which room did you come out of, Ciaran?' Mike asks cheekily.

'Mike, you asshole,' Tara says.

'Only having a laugh and being curious also. So, Ciaran, how did you sleep?'

'I slept well, thanks, Mike. Your bed is very comfy.'

He grunts and says, 'God, ye two are boring. So, are you

ready for breakfast?'

'Yeah, I am. Did you eat, Tara?' I ask.

'Oh no, I'm not long up, Mike came in around eight, he said, and started cooking.'

'Yeah, I thought ye two had a busy and late night, so I thought I would cook for ye and also I am nosy too.'

'Just for the record, Tara, I asked your family to come last night, and they all bailed. Isn't it shocking when you can't depend on anyone.' I look at Mike.

'I know, Ciaran, we're the worst. Great thing is, it didn't ruin your nice evening anyway. You got a brief experience of New York,' he says to Tara.

'I did, it was lovely. I absolutely loved it. Really felt like I was there and then we went to see Bon Jovi after sight-seeing.'

'Oh, very nice. Was he any good live?'

'Oh yeah, brilliant. Maybe we'll bring you next time,' Tara says and then looks at me.

'Oh yeah, I'd be up for that. When are you thinking? Ciaran?' he says.

'Yeah, sure, whenever suits.'

'Well, I'm staying with Tara tonight, so does tonight suit?'

'Mike, for god's sake, will you give him a break from us? I'm sure he has other plans.' Tara rolls her eyes and gets up to get a plate.

'Hey, hey, sit down. I'll get your food now,' Mike protests. 'I'm only asking. If he's not free, it's not a big deal. I just invited him to watch the concert again. If he can't, then he can't. It's called having manners, Tara.' He takes a plate and puts food on Tara's and gives it to her. 'I'll get yours next, Ciaran. So rude that the host takes the first plate.' He smirks at Tara as she puts a rasher into her mouth. She holds up a finger to him while eating the rasher.

'So, Ciaran, does it suit?' He places the plate on the table.

'Yeah, I'll let you know. My dad and I are going out with my uncle, it's his birthday, the first after his wife died. His wife would always make a big deal of his birthday so we want to mark it in some form for him. So, I'll let you know, like I'll definitely be free this evening, I just don't know what time yet.'

'*Awh*, that's nice, Ciaran, don't put pressure on yourself. If plans change, it's fine, go with the day for now,' Tara says.

'Yeah, exactly, Ciaran. I was just joking around, don't worry,' Mike says as he waves the spatula.

'No, I know, I don't feel pressured, I'll just have to let you know. So, yeah, like you said, Tara, I'll go with whatever the day brings.'

'Yeah, exactly.'

Mike brings over his plate and we all eat the fry with friendly chat.

*

I head to Tara's tonight.

I have visited her at least twice a week for the last two months. I knock at the door and Mike answers.

'Hey, Ciaran, come in. Tara doesn't feel great today,' he whispers as he closes the door.

'Oh really? I can leave and come back another day.'

'No, don't be silly, come on in. She's in the sitting room.'

I walk in and Mike is right, she seems very tired and weak today. She's sitting on the couch and has a cup of tea in her hand. She smiles when she sees me. 'Hey, Ciaran, come sit down.'

'Hey, Tara, how are you?' I sit on the chair across from the couch.

'Yeah, feel quite tired but not like sleepy tired, just fatigue, I suppose.'

'I was saying maybe we should ring the doctor,' Mike says as he stands at the door. 'But Tara says it will pass, so what can I do?'

'I'll be fine, it's just one of those days,' she says reassuringly.

'Yeah, but maybe, Mike is right, Tara. Just in case maybe it's low iron or something,' I say.

She bats her hand away. 'No, I'm fine. How are you anyway?'

'Typical Tara, doesn't want to bother anyone. Anyway, Ciaran, coffee?'

'Yeah, thanks, Mike,' I answer. He heads out to the kitchen.

'Are you sure, Tara, we shouldn't ring anyone?'

'No, honestly, it's fine. Thanks though.'

'OK, *ah*, so, I have no news really, just working and went for a drink with Megan and Tom last night. Tom sends his best and Megan too. She'll probably visit you sometime this week.'

'*Awh*, that's nice,' Tara replies.

'Yeah, so, that's all my news, very boring,' I say with a laugh.

Mike comes back with my coffee. 'Now, Ciaran, here you go.' He looks at Tara. 'Now, Queen, do you want anything?'

She smiles at Mike. 'No, fine. Thanks.'

'All right, I'll leave ye alone, I have a few phone calls to make so I'll be back into ye in a half hour. I gave ye fair warning.'

'Oh, feck off, Mike,' Tara yells.

He closes the door and gives me a wink. I hope he's messing.

'Sorry, Ciaran, he's such a prick.' She shakes her head and

laughs.

'Well, it's good to know we have a half hour without any interruption,' I say with humour.

'Oh lord, you're as bad as him.' I take a sip of my coffee and we both laugh at Mike's insinuation.

We are watching an episode of *Succession* when Mike shouts, 'I hope you are both decent, I'm coming in.' He opens the door with a grin on his face. 'Hey, you're a fast dresser, Ciaran. Fair play, so what are ye watching?'

Tara shakes her head. 'We are watching *Succession*, we wanted to watch something deceiving after what we got up to because Ciaran has a girlfriend, but she's not as pleasing as me.'

'*Ergh*, OK, I get it. Have you a woman, Ciaran?'

'No, I don't. Tara is messing with you.'

'Oh, right, anyway, I'll watch with ye, but do you want tea, sis, or coffee, Ciaran?' He looks at Tara and then at me.

'No, I'm fine, Mike, thanks,' I say.

'*Ah*, will you get me a bottle of water, please?' Tara asks.

'I'll be back,' Mike says in a terminator voice.

'*Urgh*, drive you mad,' Tara says to herself.

Mike comes back with water for Tara and another bottle for me. I take it.

'Thanks, Mike.'

'No prob. Now who is that lad, he was on some film?'

'He was on *Father of the Bride*, he's Macauley Culkin's brother,' Tara says.

'Oh yeah,' Mike answers.

The three of us stay in the sitting room chatting for hours and watching two episodes of *Succession*. Mike is going back over stories of their childhood, and I chat about mine. It's amazing that we have similar stories regarding sports, school and home life. The night has flown with all the banter and stories. Tara starts to feel tired, so she stands and tells us she's going to bed.

I offer to link her into her room, and she agrees. She feels so fragile, I gently sit her on the bed and take off her shoes and put her feet on the bed.

'Thanks, Ciaran,' Tara says as she puts her head on the pillow.

I kneel on the ground and look softly at her. I lean in, and I can't seem to control my body, I end up kissing her on the lips, 'No problem,' I say. I get up, turn off the lamp and head for the door. I look back at her and we both smile at one another, I'm not sure if it's for the tender moment or something else, but it felt nice.

*

The next morning, I'm woken by Mike, he has tears in his eyes. 'Hey, Ciaran, Tara passed.'

I jump up. 'What? But I put her to bed, how?'

'The oxygen tank was taken out of her nose, Tara never wanted to be a burden to anyone.' Mike bursts out crying.

The realisation hits me; she took it out herself.

Epilogue

I brought orange and yellow roses, I noticed they were part of her funeral cortège. I lay them down with the rest, no surprise that she has a lot of fresh flowers on her grave.

I'm about to open my mouth to talk to Tara when I'm interrupted by my name being called.

'Ciaran?' I look over and it's Helen. Wonder how often she comes here.

'Hi, Helen,' I say smiling.

'*Ah*, hi, how are you?' she asks.

'I'm good, thanks. It's strange being here, I haven't been here since her funeral.' (I lie, this is my eighth time here but first time with flowers). I am wiping a tear away from my eye, where did that come from?

'Yeah, it doesn't seem that long ago, the eight months have flown.' She exhales and looks at the grave.

'Yeah well… I'm sure they were hard months on you all.' Oh crap, another tear.

'Yeah, oh, every week was so hard.' She looks at me and continues, 'I want to say it gets easier with time, but I don't feel it yet.'

Crap, we are both crying now. The emotion of being here and being at Tara's grave, I instinctively go to hug Helen. I honestly can't move. Helen pulls away first, I am thankful she was able to pull us apart.

'Will you call sometime to us?' she asks.

'Yeah, I will, Helen, thanks.'

'Good,' she says and looks at me smiling, then wipes her eyes and I wipe mine. Helen then says, 'Oh we are both such messes, Tara would be rolling her eyes at us now.'

I burst out laughing because that is exactly what she would be doing.

*

I'm chatting up a new girl called Rose or Rosie, I can't really remember. She was good-looking across the bar, but she can talk for Ireland. All I wanted was a few pleasantries and then back to mine, but it looks like she's a talker and that's not good for me because that means she will want my number, stay awhile the next morning, and want to meet again. It's time now for me to excuse myself and go to another pub.

AH, yes! This place is better, it's quite crowded so plenty of selection. I look around and see a woman in a pink string top and black skirt. I go over with the usual chat up lines, and she is soaking them all in, this will be easy. Another successful night for Ciaran.